Strax and the Widow
The Society Trilogy, Volume 1

Victoria L. Szulc

Copyright © 2012, 2014, 2020, 2022 Victoria L. Schultz/Hen Publishing, a Hen Companies Brand

All rights reserved. Although there are references to actual historic events, places, and people, all of the characters, places, and dialogue in this book and its related stories, are fictitious, and any resemblance to any person living, dead, or undead is coincidental.

A gentle word to my readers/trigger warning: *although my pieces are works of fiction, my books and stories contain scenes and depictions that may upset certain audiences.*

Cover Art Direction/Photography: Victoria L. Szulc

Graphic Design: Michele Berhorst

Model: Ashley Meyer

ISBN-13: 978-1-958760-02-4

FOR THE BRAVE ONES.

They are not without fear but summon the courage
to rise in the most dire situations and
dare to succeed in the face of adversity.

ACKNOWLEDGMENTS

Special thanks to my family, friends, and fans who have journeyed with me through many changes.

PROLOGUE-IRIS

Iris, Texas – August 1895

How did this happen? Katherine Church stepped out from a run-down saloon. She adjusted her brown short-brimmed gambler hat to guard against a blinding mid-sun. A dry wind tickled her blond curly tendrils as she focused. With leather gloved hands, she tugged down her welding goggles over her oval-shaped face to protect her still bright blue eyes. She prepared to fight more than just the high noon glare.

Kate, as most knew her, smoothed over her weather-beaten brown leather coat that extended past her knees, covered her womanly frame, and hid a secret weapon. She double-checked that her handmade pistol was within reach, tucked neatly just below her right hip. The gun was peculiar, put together from various parts. A fluorescent green liquid replaced the purpose of gun powder. She was prepared to bet her life on the unique piece.

A foolish, drunken cowboy tumbled out of the saloon behind her, bolstered to fight by alcohol and the goading of a truly evil man. That despicable being, Drasco, stood at the end of the porch of the watering hole and leered in her direction.

The miscreant had just been coerced into the gun battle by a spur-of-the-moment scheme initiated by Drasco. Kate's new adversary shuffled along as his boots raised mini dust devils in his wake.

Breathe, you are strong. Kate reminded herself of the lessons friends taught her. They were praying for her, hoping that heaven offered protection. Anxiety coiled in her belly like a rattlesnake ready to strike.

Why do I have to be the hero? Kate detested violence. She pretended not to see Drasco's glare and set her sights on the task at hand.

I'm making the best shot possible, she resolved with a deep inhale of Texas wind.

The onlookers were so riveted at the impending gunfight, that they didn't notice that Kate was wearing a man's winter duster during the summer. She was of average height, five-foot-six, but every inch of it was ready to tangle with a rotten outlaw. Her gut twisted in anticipation. She bristled at having to kill this man, but Kate was forced into it. She ignored the sweat that trickled along the nape of her neck. The growing crowd hoped to see justice served.

I can't let them down.

It was a ragtag group of villagers that came to watch the conflict. Farming families scattered about the aging doorways of the rotting buildings. The blowing dust dirtied the faces of impatient children.

Their weary mothers continually adjusted their hats and caps, attempting to keep them clean. The fathers wore beat-up shirts and trousers; they barely earned enough to put food on the table, let alone get new duds. The best wear was saved for Sunday services. Today was a day for someone to die. It wasn't necessary to be well attired.

Other folks—the general storekeeper, the saloon owner, cowpokes, travelers, and a band of suspicious characters—lined the street. A young Catholic nun, Sister Theresa, collected three of her charges and shuffled them away from the impending violence. Her habit blew in the wind and covered the look of concern that shadowed her brow. Rising fear caused her hands to quiver as she hurried the children along.

The crowd shuffled impatiently. Pocket watches were checked. Tension mounted as the onlookers waited for the whistle of the train. It had become the official harbinger of street justice in Iris.

It was one of those blistering dry days in the near-desert that sucked the moisture out of all living things. Iris, Texas had once been a pleasant stop to the Wild West. It was a boom town on the first rail line through the immense state. Iris was filled with ranchers, prospectors, and railmen before the Civil War. Now, the trains seemed to be the only business that kept the forsaken place alive. Most departed further West, to richer lands. But this hell hole stayed aloft as a stop along a desolate stretch, providing fuel, entertainment, food, and libations to whoever arrived off the train.

Guests didn't stay long now. Jobs rolled on with the rails. When trains and cattle drives vacated the town, Main Street was empty enough that even the sounds of lightly treading horses echoed off the vacated buildings that decayed in the sun. Those structures still contained businesses, with only necessary staff on call to serve guests. Iris was a good place to hide and a bad place to stay too long. The marauders and vagrants that became frequent visitors to Iris, gave the local ranchers reasons to be concerned. Their herds began to disappear, mysteriously, little by little.

Kate had overstayed. She'd earned her tough reputation after residing in Iris for twenty years. How she'd remained alive was a testament to her will to live despite a violent past and a soft heart that longed for the promise of better days. She didn't have a plan when she'd come to Iris years ago. She was more focused on getting away from her past than running to her future.

Those coming days were murky. At present, Kate was still gainfully employed by the railroad, a job that brought her here. She was part of a handful of employees left. The trains came twice a day, at noon and five in the eve. They delivered and picked up the mail, carried supplies for the general store, and brought prosperity to town through prospectors and gamblers. The saloon was still open, its plush surroundings fueled by alcohol, a final oasis of entertainment.

Townspeople came to the saloon's Saturday night poker game as their last chance to act as a community and to perhaps gain a fortune. They were increasingly joined by wayward ranchers and vagabond gamblers hustling to create fools out of those present. Players were old war veterans, naïve farmers, and stubborn ranchers who stayed because there was nowhere else to go. Lovely ladies kept the eccentric bunch entertained as long as they purloined enough money for drinks. Unfortunately, it was also a frequent source of fights and standoffs which often led to trouble outside. A recent incident was the reason Kate was ready to draw.

Soon a duel would explode in front of that saloon.

I cannot believe what has happened here. Kate recalled as she prepared herself. Her competitor was taking his time, strolling towards his end of the main drag. She blinked behind her goggles and let her mind relax. She hesitated before moving out into the street and remembered how wonderful Iris was when she'd first arrived.

Strax and the Widow

CONTENTS

	Acknowledgments	iv
	Prologue-Iris	v
1	Arrival	12
2	A Desert Life	23
3	Ancient Wisdom	36
4	Shootout	53
5	The Widow	74
6	The First Invitation	76
7	Wounds	89
8	A Gentleman Comes	120
9	A Swim and Friendly Games of Poker	126
10	Intervention	141
11	Branded	147
12	Boom	155
13	A Kidnapping and an Offer	166
14	Exodus	175
15	Nacogdoches	181
16	The Circus	196
17	Home	211

1 ARRIVAL

Iris, Texas - 1876

When Kate Church arrived in the bustling town of Iris, the railroad tracks were still under swift construction. Scarcely sixteen, Kate ran to where opportunities existed, the wild west. She was forced to leave St. Louis, a river and beer boomtown of its own. Horrible events had transpired.

The consequences were grave. She had vacated in a flash, garbed in a simple dark blue gown, gathered tight at the waist, sparingly trimmed with matching lace and bonnet.

Kate jumped off the noon train and withdrew from attention. She hid off to the side of the depot with her chin drawn in, shoulders hunched, and let the other passengers whisk past her.

A throng of travelers hurried about the platform as conductors validated tickets and coachmen picked up their charges. Boots clattered over the wooden planks. Horses kicked up dust as they waited impatiently for their drivers. Everyone seemed to know where they were headed. Kate stood in awe of the busy town in front of her.

The spectacle of livestock running in the street, drunken cowboys stumbling about and the undertaker propping up a dead soldier for a last photo on the porch of the barber shop, overwhelmed Kate. The view made her shiver, even in the heat. She took a deep breath to appease her frayed nerves. She clutched her baggage tightly while her heart pounded in her chest as if it would leap out into the street.

The young Katherine Church was a wisp of an adolescent, with wide blue eyes and porcelain skin. She'd tucked her blonde ringlets into a mature bun to appear old enough to be in a proper office. She was educated and appropriately garbed. She desperately required the employment that she'd found far from home.

Back in St. Louis, Kate found an ad in the paper for railroad workers of all sorts, from secretaries to steel men. Go west young man, was the cry then. It became her calling too, for she was hired by the railroad and sent to Texas.

Kate was carrying only a satchel and a leather trunk when she jostled a petite oriental woman on the train platform. The wild sights of the town distracted her.

"Cart? I have cart, see?" The Asian lady chattered.

"No, no...I have it, that's alright." Kate stuttered and straightened herself as her eyes adjusted to the desert sun.

"I help, no charge," the foreign woman insisted in broken English. She piled Kate's wares on top of a closed basket in a cart that was led by a gray, rugged donkey. "I Ming, where you go Miss?" she inquired. Ming squinted at the fair-haired young woman. She ran a bony crooked finger over her chin.

The Asian felt Kate would be in trouble if she stayed on the platform too long. The newcomer looked like a lost child clutching her favorite doll. Insidious folk passing through a new town like Iris would take advantage of a naive adolescent like Kate. The kind-hearted washer woman worried for the sweet girl. She didn't seem like the other painted ladies that arrived in Iris. Far too many of them ended up as whores or saloon girls.

"I—I'm searching for the rail office," Kate stammered, still startled at the rush around the train. Her fingers ached from clutching her luggage too tightly. She wrung her now empty hands in anticipation.

"Over there, see, we go." Ming glanced nervously as the crowd thinned out. "It not good we stay here long. Girl like you, easy pickings they say. Come now. You with the rail?" Ming clucked like a mother hen as she led Kate to an outbuilding aside from the train station, its construction still in process with piles of wood and tools scattered about. "I am Ming, I clean clothes." They stopped about ten feet from the door of the rail office and unloaded Kate's items. Ming was relieved that Kate had a place to go. She'd seen children discarded like rubbish. Travelers were so desperate to find their fortunes westward, that they left children behind, dumping them at train stops along the way. Enough orphans required assistance, that Sisters from a nearby Mission opened a home in town to tend to the needy children. Ming didn't have children of her own, but she despised those who neglected their young.

"Yes, I am working for the railroad." Kate wondered at her miniature savior. "I'm Miss Katherine Church. Thank you for your services." Kate dug in her bag for payment, but Ming shook her head and covered Kate's hand.

"No, Miss Church, you keep, okay?" Ming's broken English tumbled through her petite mouth. Ming was grateful that Kate was kind to her despite her Asian descent. Most weren't kind to the slanty-eyed folk. They were good enough to work the rails and do laundry but weren't welcome at most of Iris's new businesses.

"Yes indeed, good day." Kate smiled back and paused, then added, "And you can call me Kate."

"Good day, Kate," Ming bowed and led her donkey away into town to gather laundry from the rail staff.

Kate watched her hustle away and then turned her attention to the building. She gulped as her knuckles rapped on the office door. *I must do this.*

The first of a long line of rail supervisors, a Mr. Smith, opened the door wearing a dirty undershirt, suspenders, and ill-fitting trousers. A cigar hung on his hairy lip, and his bald head gleamed in the sun from perspiration. A pair of wrinkly eyes looked her up and down. "What do ya want, missy?" he growled.

"I'm Miss Katherine Church. The railroad has offered me a secretarial position?" She stared at the grimy character who would briefly manage her.

"Oh yeah, come on in, darlin'," he muttered grimly. In passing him into the office, Kate smelled the distinct sting of whisky on his breath. She entered the dimly lit space which lacked organization. Piles of books, papers, a couple of bottles of half-empty liquor, and even tools were scattered about the tiny room. Two heavy pine desks were buried in mounds of papers, their matching chairs peeking out from behind the mess. He brought them to the center of the room, offered her a seat, and grabbed parchment, a pen, and ink from the top of the stacks.

"Well then, I have enough to keep you busy, see? You'll be here each day, from nine until the five o'clock train pulls out. You'll hear its whistle, and then you know you can go for the day. I don't like tardiness. See, the rail folk get here at sunup, leave at sundown. And in between, we've got all kinds of paperwork and bookkeeping. You think you can bring order to this mess?" He sloppily chewed on the cigar.

"Yes sir, I'll do the best I can." Kate faked confidence but was so overwhelmed at the disarrayed room, that her voice trembled.

"Alright then," he drawled. "You can begin tomorrow. As promised, you get your room and board at the smaller hotel for a week or two. After that, you'll be needin' to find a place to stay. This ain't nothing fancy. You can bring your dinner pail or get sundries at the general store. Remember, nine sharp. Don't be late." He tapped Kate on the shoulder and then escorted her out. "See you tomorrow, Miss Church. Be ready to work." The door clattered shut behind Kate.

She stood alone outside the rail office, afraid of what the future would bring. She gingerly wiped an irritating sweat from her brow with a delicate handkerchief, calmed her fluttering heart, and strode towards the better hotels in town.

This initial meeting began a series of hard days, layers of bookkeeping, and multiple office managers. Each morning, for the next two months, when she'd arrive, Mr. Smith would be nursing a hang-over from the night before yet swilling on a fresh bottle of liquor. Kate wrote letters, filed, and accounted for whatever had to be tended to. Then she'd tackle the backlog of books and papers. Mr. Smith tracked in and out of the office during the day, checked on rail men, ordered supplies, visited the post, smoked cigars, and enjoyed generous swigs of whisky. By the end of the day, he was barely literate, but not dangerous—just sleepy drunk.

He'd leered her over but was never rude with her. Like most, he couldn't afford to lose this job. Mr. Smith realized this girl that the railroad hired was pretty, and she seemed dignified unlike most of the ladies that passed through. He wondered why Kate chose to come there, of all places. He'd come in and catch her staring off on occasion. Mr. Smith surmised she was probably reminiscing, but it didn't matter. She was here now. She'd cleaned up the place, procured fabric from Ming the cleaning lady, and made fresh curtains. He managed to keep the riff-raff out of the office and let her toil in peace.

Things were going well for the odd pair of rail workers until the morning that Kate walked in to find Mr. Smith face down at his desk.

Surely, he's drunk too much liquor and just fell asleep. She crossed the room to wake him and touched a cold shoulder. She tapped him, then prodded aloud. "Mr. Smith, Mr. Smith?" He was motionless, having died in the chair shortly after closing the day before. Kate leaned back with her hand over her mouth at the realization he departed from this earth.

"Oh my God!" She burst outside and ran directly to the sheriff.

She trembled inside the doorway of his office. "Sir, sheriff. Um, I think Mr. Smith is dead.

The sheriff peered up from his desk and a half-eaten plate of eggs and bacon. "What's that? Dead?"

"Yes," Kate whispered.

"Well then, let's get the doc. And the undertaker." The sheriff wiped his lips with plump fingers and rose. He was a portly man who hardly walked let alone run.

He and Kate called on the town doctor and the undertaker. The motley crew stopped to pick up a rail foreman, Mr. Riley, on the way back to the office.

"Mr. Riley, Sir. I—I think—" Kate stuttered as they rushed through the rail yard.

"Your office manager has bit the dust. We may need you. Can't tell how many men it'd take to lift the body." The undertaker chortled.

"But we have to find out if he's dead." The doc chimed in.

"Alright then." Riley tossed his tools aside and they marched onto the office.

Once they assembled inside, the doctor leaned over and felt around Mr. Smith's cold neck.

"Yep, he's a goner." The doc sighed as the undertaker covered him with a blanket.

Warm tears spilled down Kate's cheeks as she wept aloud.

"Now, now, Missy. You go on home. These fellows will get Mr. Smith's final rest taken care of." The sheriff put an arm around Kate and led her out the door.

The foreman followed, his furrowed brow revealing his care for this new young woman in the office. She was a hard worker. He was concerned that this death would scare her off.

"Come back tomorrow, we'll sort this out. I'll wire the main office to send a new manager."

The rail did send a fresh manager a couple of weeks after Mr. Smith was buried. They sent several managers, over and over. Each time a new one would come in; he'd be too big for his britches in the little town. He'd get drunk, get into trouble, get fired, or quit.

Kate continued to keep the office in order. Most of her tasks were done by eleven each day and then she would read or write letters. The railroad continued to pay decently, and she'd send funds home to her father and Abby, her younger sister.

As the season turned to winter, Kate was between office managers and effective at running the office on her own. With the cold coming in, Kate fired up the office stove only to find the flue was clogged. She'd begun tinkering with it just as Mr. Riley came in.

"Can you fix things, Miss Church? We ain't got time to fill these oil lamps and I have other equipment that could use fixin'. It would mean additional pay for you." He was impressed with her determination and her abilities for a lady of her age.

"I'd be glad to try." Kate agreed. The foreman always treated her respectfully and she looked forward to learning from him.

Mr. Riley trained Kate on mechanical repairs and passed on plenty of extra duties. Word spread about her talents. In short order, she was running water and tools to the men, serving slop, and cleaning machine parts. In between jobs, he would encourage her with gentle taps on her shoulder and kind words. "You're doing a fine job."

The extra money she earned went a long way.

"All the way at the end. Wasn't used much except to store junk. Rent due first of the month." A raspy-voiced saloon manager tossed keys to Kate as she upgraded from a closet-sized room at the hotel to accommodations above the saloon. She bustled down a long empty hall from where the dancing girls slept and socialized with the male visitors. A set of stairs along the outside of the saloon led to her door. It was originally designed to allow easy access.

"This will do." She whispered as she unloaded her sparse collection of clothes. Kate liked the outer entry, as she avoided the saloon and its squalor entirely. The room provided her with privacy from the bustling town with just enough space for a wire frame bed, washstand, and closet.

In those first few months, Kate's body continuously ached from the hard labor. Most days she'd have just enough strength to wipe down and go to bed. She didn't have the energy to mix with other folk and preferred to save her earnings.

Mr. Riley, after learning that Kate was alone in Iris, took a liking to her in a fatherly way. He became her protector from the young hellions who drank liberally, gambled away what they earned, and were seeking companionship at the end of a hard day. "Let's grab a bite." He offered to share his lunch pail and would wave off any wayward suitors that wanted to join them for a meal.

Mr. Riley was a gray-haired widower who worked with the trains from their birth, tinkering with the steam engines, the wheels, and the fixtures inside the stately, expensive cars. He was a tall, solid man from serving the rails and served in the Northern infantry in the Civil War.

He had kind brown eyes and was decently groomed for a rail man with his peppered, well-trimmed goatee. His wife passed at a young age from a sort of pox before they'd ever had children. Although he'd been alone since then, the rails kept him happy. Riley, as everyone called him, had never been a proper upper-crust gentleman, but he'd acted like one. He was a stern foreman, yet courteous. Occasionally he'd send Kate to get sweets from the general store for the orphans that wandered into the office and were curious about the trains.

When another young fool failed to show up to fix lamps in the cars, Riley recruited Kate. He stood at the door of the office as she tidied up. "Ready to do different work?"

"Yes Sir!" Kate threw on a bonnet and followed Riley out to the workshop near the tracks.

To his delight, she was a fast learner, not leery of using tools and her smaller hands could get into tight spaces. She possessed a gift around horses too, carrying a whip and later buying a fine steed of her own, Sonny. Eventually, she was slinging her tool belt and learning to weld simple repairs.

He recognized her naivety in dealing with the fellas. Riley protected her from getting caught up with the dance hall girls and gamblers. He taught her wisdom beyond the office and rails, keeping her clear of the mayhem that would happen after hours.

After ripping the only dress she owned, Riley brought her trousers, shirt, and suspenders from the general store. "You'll always be a lady Kate," he handed her the clothes, "but this is suited to what I'll be needin' you for. You can always buy yourself a new dress."

"Thanks, Riley." Kate was grateful as the searing hot summer turned her clothes into rags. Sweat ruined her undergarments despite their multiple cleanings from Ming.

Kate enjoyed her interactions with Ming and her husband Chin. They were older folk who lacked employment on the East coast. They got on the railroad west for brighter futures. As Kate filled laundry carts, she enjoyed the stories of their past. "We stop in towns that get big fast. Long train lines to build and still building! We meet all kinds. Rich ladies in pearls and velvet. Freed slaves and people of Europe. We see a big horse off a big ship. Big bump on back. They say it a camel from far away, over big ocean."

Her hands gestured to the immense size of the foreign animal. Ming's enthusiasm and tales of the railroad made Kate giggle and wonder about the world outside of Iris.

Ming did laundry as Chin toiled in the rail yards until he became too old for the heavy tasks. They lived out of a pitched tent at each stop near whatever water they found. They weren't accepted among the wealthy, but the way they washed clothes kept them busy and prosperous among the workers. They were seen about town with their laundry cart piled high with baskets of the nasty-smelling vestiges of the rail men. They'd hustle their loads down to the creek and clean clothes, rags, and linens most of the day. They didn't speak perfect English, but it didn't matter to Kate and Riley. They were talented and trustworthy. They translated for the other Chinese rail staff and ensured that pay was distributed.

Working for the rail was prosperous then. After a few years, Kate afforded a flowered print dress for church and an exquisite black satin dress. The dark gown was a rare extravagance. Its high collar with a ruffled trim grazed her chin. The covered buttons down the front enhanced her bust and waistline. The layered bustle and train gave her hips and the desired backside. She'd ordered it, along with a parasol, after seeing it in a catalog at the general store. One day, while picking up basic supplies for the rail office, she'd finally earned enough money to purchase the goods.

I'll never wear it, so impractical, except, well, for darker days, I suppose. She'd put it aside for a day when she could afford to go to a civilized town or return home. The dress, hidden behind more suitable garments in her closet, kept her spirits up. As those first years in the town passed, Kate still dreamed of a life in a genteel city, of lavender soaps and china, of well-heeled ladies, and gentlemen in fine carriages.

Strax and the Widow

2 A DESERT LIFE

Iris, Texas - Early 1880's

"Now Kate, hold her steady and remember to breathe. Get to the center of your target, not just the edge." Riley's warm voice tickled Kate's ear as she aimed a rifle at a set of bottles lined up on a rickety line of wooden plank fencing.

They were far outside of Iris for additional firearms training. Riley became her mentor in all things mechanical. "Now fire," he whispered hoarsely.

When Kate pulled the trigger, the weapon shuddered through her bones. The targeted bottle blew to smithereens. Kate smirked at her teacher.

Riley chuckled. "Now don't get too cocky, little lady. Tomorrow we're taking those bottles further out."

Kate grew along with Iris. She'd become a lovely young woman in her twenties, even under the rough rail wear. Men teased her, often in rude ways, to Riley's ire. Kate managed to deflect their interest in the beginning.

But as the population of Iris increased, so did the number of its rowdier inhabitants. Riley's concern for Kate's safety increased, as did the unwelcomed attention which was now a daily occurrence. Appreciating Kate's independence, Riley planned days like these to sharpen her gun-slinging skills. He handled the men that were employed under him; the strangers in town were another matter. He trained her so that she could defend herself with firepower.

"Okay, focus now. Let's go for those three. Do 'em right in a row, bam, bam, bam," Riley ordered briskly.

Kate took her mark and shattered the bottles in swift succession.

"Oh, my goodness, that was amazing," Kate lowered the rifle.

"I pray you never have to use these," Riley muttered while taking the weapon from her. He despised having to teach a woman how to be violent, but it was necessary. "We'll practice and go on a hunt, that way you'll get an idea of how to hit a moving target. Rifles are meant for the military, hunting, and long-range shooting. Or heaven forbid when you can't afford to miss."

Kate listened. She'd been afraid of guns, but now with Riley's guidance, she was skilled at using a pistol and progressed on to larger weapons.

Riley took on a cheerier tone. It was getting late in the afternoon and evenings were lonely for the rail folk of Iris.

"Why don't you show me how your whip is coming along?" he called back to her as he cleaned up the broken glass.

Kate snatched up her favorite tool from a weather-beaten shoulder bag. The eight-foot black bull whip was one of the scant items she'd brought to Iris. The letters "MP" were embossed into a thick piece of leather on the handle. In ranching and farming, country whips were indispensable. Kate made a wise choice in keeping it close. At home in St. Louis, she'd become quite skilled in using it. Over time, she'd taught Riley a thing or two, and even made him a couple of custom pieces.

"How'd you learn to make and crack whips so well?" Riley was curious as to how such a petite gal got such talent.

Kate blushed. "A family friend taught me." After observing her obvious discomfort, Riley backed off.

"Alright then, what are you showing me today?" Riley teased.

"Well, four corners. Put a bottle at each of the four points of the compass," Kate commanded.

Riley mused that the Western bottle location would be directly in line with the setting sun. He wondered if she'd be able to see.

"Alright then." He placed the targets on the dirty desert floor as requested and retreated.

Kate stood in the center of her glass prey. Her eyes darted to each target. With a sweeping motion like that of a lithe snake, Kate raised her arm and snapped her weapon in broad, quick loops. She made slight, unperceivable turns as the whip took out each bottle.

If the sunset blinded her, Riley couldn't tell. The Western bottle shattered like the rest.

Riley was amazed at her expertise. "Miss Church, that was extraordinary I'd say."

"Really?" Kate laughed. She coiled and hooked her weapon to her belt. "I had a decent teacher, you know." Kate gazed off into the setting golden orb. Riley hated these moments. Kate did her best to hide her melancholy feelings.

Riley pried. "Kate, did that man who showed you, well, uh…did he hurt you?" He hated being invasive, but he loved Kate like a daughter. Anyone that hurt her would have to contend with his wrath.

Kate groaned. *I can never tell*, she reminded herself. To reveal her past, put her family in jeopardy. But each night before sleep, Kate still fondly recalled the young man who'd taught her. She swallowed hard at the memories.

"No, he was a good man. He never hurt anyone. He's been gone a long time now." Kate choked back tears. "Riley, I hope you understand why I can't say anymore." Her shadowy frame turned to the West as he put a comforting arm around her.

"You loved him though?" Riley prodded.

"Yes." Kate's voice was pained.

"It's not wrong to love, Kate." She was stubborn for someone so young, Riley pondered. He pressed on. "You know it's not too late for you to meet a kind man."

Kate cut him off abruptly. "No. I have a family that relies on me. I have to be here right now. I can't be distracted by all sorts of silliness." She straightened away from his gentle embrace.

"All right then. Let's go back and get supper then?" Riley soothed and marveled at her resolve.

"Yes, this activity has me quite famished," Kate spoke with a ladylike demeanor. She resisted the urge to tell Riley what happened back in St. Louis. But he didn't need to know her past. He just needed to know that she trusted him with everything else.

A few months earlier

"You can use this space as you like." Riley handed her the key to the railyard tool shed.

Once settled in Iris, Kate was delighted to have her own space to repair rail equipment and tinker in her spare time. Kate built practical items, like clocks and furniture. She even made a better washboard for Ming in trade for laundry services.

The wooden building was lined with shelving and a multitude of tools. A sturdy bench became Kate's creation table. And then there were the guns.

First Kate learned how to clean and repair them. With Riley's guidance, she constructed firearms from spare parts.

"Impressive, Kate. Remember to stay armed and keep these newfound skills to yourself." Riley advised.

"Will do." Kate gave a freshly refurbished pistol a cursory glance and packed up for the night.

"The element of surprise is one of your best tools. Never forget." His words would be ingrained in Kate's mind forever.

Kate's talents weren't the only concerns she kept close to the vest. She held onto the secrets of her past. Discretion served her well.

Three years after her arrival, Kate was waiting for the noon train at the post. As the locomotive rolled to a stop, a familiar man hustled onto the platform. Her heart crashed at full recognition of the brother of a former betrothed.

What is he doing here?

He was searching for a girl, showing a sketch to guests on the platform. Kate gasped.

No doubt that's a picture of me.

Seven years had passed since she had last seen Peter McKendrick, and he was still as repulsive as her former forced fiancé. Although Kate was twenty-four at the time of this run-in, she froze as the memories of her past with this visitor's brother haunted her.

Dear God, please don't let him see me.

She shouldn't have stressed. Kate was barely recognizable from her adolescent days, and she was dressed entirely in men's clothes.

With a deep breath, she crept inside the post, collected the mail, and discreetly spied as most of the passengers and townsfolk passed McKendrick by. The train departed, but disappointment set in as the wretched man didn't leave.

Why didn't he go?

McKendrick strode over to where teams of men packed up their shipments.

"You see this girl?" McKendrick shoved a paper in a rail worker's hands.

"Hey, can't you see we're busy?" Riley shooed the interloper away from his team. "We haven't got time for questions. This load of equipment and supplies has to be out in a half-hour. Try the saloon or the sheriff." Riley hissed. People always went missing in the West. The visitor wasn't offering anything in exchange for information, which made his questioning even less desirable.

Fate was on Kate's side that day. Ranchers called the sheriff out to question a suspected cattle thief, so McKendrick couldn't ask him. As a weary McKendrick left the jail and shuffled off to a saloon where he made inquiries, Kate hustled back to the office. It wasn't long before cheating vagrants drew Mr. McKendrick in for drinks and a long game of afternoon poker.

Kate bided her time in the rail office as rumors spread around that an inquisitive interloper lost loads of cash at the saloon late that afternoon. He was so dejected that he left on the 5 o'clock train out.

As the whistle blew, and the rail staff scrambled home, Kate sighed with relief.

At last.

Mr. McKendrick continued to hunt for Kate as he lost at poker in small-town stops on the rail line. At the end of a particularly drunken game in California, he lost his life to a sore loser.

Months later, fortune provided Kate with closure. As she gathered mail, she picked up a discarded paper from gold rush country that a passenger left behind at the post. Kate flicked through its battered pages hungry for news out West. She scanned the obituaries and was relieved to find the insidious bastard's demise. With a satisfied "Hmmph," she tossed the paper into an ash pit, "he's never coming back." Kate felt light as a feather.

Anxiety-ridden nights ended once Kate had discovered that McKendrick perished.

Trains were the lifeblood of Iris. Their steady rhythm of arrival and departure was a pleasant constant. The rail company prospered for another eight years despite its consistent change of management. Kate was thirty-two when a young manager, Ferris Tomley, arrived and brought stability to the office.

"Welcome to the Iris rail office." Kate greeted Ferris. "You must be Mr. Tomley." She gazed over the light-skinned gentleman who appeared to be in his early twenties.

He was of medium height, had an attractive full head of black curly hair, and a matching groomed mustache. A bit of a dandy, he wore studious glasses near the tip of his nose and was impeccably dressed for a man that was employed by the railroad.

"Yes, I am." Ferris eyed his new secretary. She was outfitted in a man's shirt, overalls, and boots. "And you must be Miss Church?"

"Yes sir, pleased to meet you." Kate slipped off a battered leather glove to shake the hand of her new manager. "You can set your bags down here." Kate waved to his desk. "Let's go for a walk outside and I'll introduce you to the foreman, Mr. Riley."

As they strolled out into a hot summer morning, Ferris adjusted his jacket and spectacles. A trembling hand smoothed over his hair before he replaced his bowler. He was unnerved at the attractive woman who would be his office girl. Kate strode into the rail yard and ignored the dirty smirks of those that yearned for even a piece of her. Upon spotting Mr. Riley fixing the lock on a boxcar, she called.

"We have our new manager, Mr. Riley." Kate motioned.

Mr. Riley scrambled over rail ties and eagerly welcomed the new manager with a slapping handshake. "Mr. Riley, at your service, sir. Welcome to Iris."

"Thank you kindly." Ferris was comforted by a qualified number of men busily working on all sorts of equipment and no malcontents. "It seems like you have quite a crew here." He exhaled and again adjusted his spectacles.

"Well, been quite a few changes at the office. We're sure to keep it simple and productive out here. I'll fill you in once you get settled." Mr. Riley tipped his hat.

"I'll be happy to go over our most recent paperwork in a moment after I assist Mr. Riley with this piece of machinery." Kate held a selection of gears in her hand. "If you'd like, Mr. Tomley, you can go to unpack?"

"I will, thank you both." Ferris trotted to the office, happy that he'd been placed at an efficient depot.

Kate and Riley watched their new manager slip into the rail office.

"By the looks of him in those fine clothes, I give him two, maybe three weeks." Riley snickered.

"Are we placing bets, then?" Kate bantered back. "Here, you can have these." She handed the parts to the foreman, laughed, and returned to the office as Ferris' demeanor played in her mind.

This manager is different. Doesn't smell like liquor. Sounds educated. Maybe he'll stick around.

Within hours of his arrival, the local females had heard of the new man in town. Gossip spread like wildfire. But Ferris paid no mind to them. He was instantly intrigued with Kate.

It wasn't long before Ferris secretly fancied her strength, her gifts at repairing mechanical items for the rail, and how she wore trousers. It was oddly enrapturing for him to see a woman look lovely in male attire. She was ten years older than he but was drawn to her vivaciousness and pluck. He'd admired how hard she saved for her family. How she hadn't seen them in years, but dutifully wrote each week.

Since the first day in Iris, when Kate showed him around town and the office, Ferris felt a pleasant warmth in her presence.

Kate was a mature woman when Ferris arrived. Despite her tanned skin, she'd remained youthful and developed a lady's figure. Her full bosom and buttocks would still be apparent, even in men's clothing. The workers would whistle or tease, but she easily put them down with quick wit and charm. Kate was stubborn and dismissive to these fools, but she secretly yearned for a gentleman to make her a proper lady. Those dreams faded as time moved on, like the backside of the caboose that left the town station.

Kate developed a simple life. She worked on the rails Monday through Saturday and kept Ferris on his toes. Away from the office, she'd tinker in the shed, practice weaponry with Riley, visit Ming and Chin, or ride her horse, Sonny. Before bed, Kate would settle in with scripture or a newspaper. She'd stroke her whip over the embossed handle, hang it on the bedpost before dreaming of the past, and fall into a deep slumber.

On Sundays, Kate blossomed. She liked Sundays for the simple fact that she wore a dress to church.

The holy building was set a ways from town. The wooden planks of the walls were whitewashed over by its parishioners. A tiny cross at the top point of its steeple beckoned the Christian faithful.

Kate prayed for the safety of her friends and family in solitude. She found peace among the sturdy oak pews, away from the business of Iris. She gazed at its paned windows and admired the desert beauty. The Father listened to her confessions as Kate unburdened her soul. Inside, Kate was still a refined woman even if the leather fashion she usually wore demonstrated otherwise.

Kate did gain an unexpected male to share her desert life with. On a rainy autumn morning, Riley burst through the office doors.

"Got a surprise for you, Miss Kate." Riley let a medium-sized stray mutt galivant into the room, his muddy paws splattering the wood floor. "This fella was wandering on the station platform. Here's a rope to tether him by."

"What is this?" Kate rose from her desk. The pooch came to her and sat at her feet. She leaned over and caressed his forehead. "Who is this character?"

"He was lost, but now he's found," Riley joked. "Left behind for greener pastures I suppose."

"He's left a mess," Ferris chided at the dirty paw prints.

"That is easily cleaned. Maybe not for his ear though." Kate peered into the beast's left ear as he winced. A notch in the fur was lined with dried blood on the inside. "I think he's had a tumble. I'll have to get a closer look." With soft hands, Kate soaked a clean rag in fresh water, wiped the injury clean, and bandaged the ear. Her new friend swiped at it with a nagging paw, but with a stern "No" and a strip jerky from his new owner, the dog took repose at the side of Kate's desk.

Although he was miffed at the mess the canine made, upon witnessing this pleasant exchange, Ferris' fondness for Miss Church grew.

Kate trained her new four-legged friend well. He always accompanied Kate, including trips to the general store. During his first visit, he was dubbed "Strax" after one of the town's toddler orphans noted the dog pawing at his ear.

"Strax! Strax!" The child's eyes widened with delight at the sight of the dog. Kate stopped on the porch to let the child and Sister Theresa pass. The dog took the moment to loosen the bandage.

"What is he saying?" Kate laughed.

"He can't say scratch." Sister Theresa giggled.

The child pointed at the canine, "Strax, Strax!"

The dog stopped his grooming upon hearing the child's sweet outburst and trotted to the boy. He began to lick the entranced infant.

Sister Theresa grinned. "I think your dog has a new friend."

"Indeed, he does." Kate kneeled and joined the group on the ground. And so, the name Strax stuck on Kate's dog.

Strax was her constant companion, even sitting beside the outhouse when she'd go to relieve herself.

His head came conveniently to her hip where Kate's hand playfully petted his spanking white fur near the black spot around his right eye.

Strax's square jaw made him appear tougher than he was. The damaged ear healed but left a rough scar. He'd have a go at it, even after his initial treatments.

"Hmmph, let's get a closer look." Kate's examination revealed further injury, the ear was probably infected long ago, and it appeared to have affected his hearing. "I've got an idea."

Kate researched new hearing devices that elderly folk were using. Before long, she'd created a special attachment for Strax.

"Let's try this." Kate strapped a mechanical cone contraption to the damaged ear. "Better?"

Strax barked with recognition of his elevated hearing capabilities. "This will be better than before the injury." Kate consoled with long smooth pats on Strax's back.

Riley was pleased to see Kate warm to Strax. When he found Strax wandering the platform, he realized that the dog might be additional protection for Kate. The rail foreman cheated time and was living a longer life than most. But he was getting on in years and did what he could to assist Kate. It wasn't ideal for a woman to be alone this long. She was far from a spinster, but the town was changing. It would be wise for her to have a sidekick.

In the present, people were leaving Iris rather than staying. Those that remained were an undesirable lot.

"Don't send it all back home, Kate. Save a little for yourself." He reminded.

"You shouldn't worry so much." She'd reply.

He recognized the faraway look in her eyes. It was too late for him to leave, but not for her. Iris was changing and it wasn't going to be for the better.

3 ANCIENT WISDOM

Iris, Texas – 1892

"I'm beginning to detest Saturdays," Kate grumbled as fired railmen spewed profanities and imbibed copious amounts of alcohol in the yard. "Gonna be a mess tomorrow. How many were let go?"

"Five this round." Ferris reviewed the termination orders that the railroad sent via telegram. Saturday became the day when he'd distribute the walking papers and remaining pay for the less fortunate staff. "Don't pay no mind to it, Kate. I'll handle it."

Despite his initial impression of Kate and Riley, Ferris turned out to be an astute and fair manager. He gave Riley a heads up on who was leaving, so he could attempt to cushion the blow to the men in his charge.

Kate eavesdropped on their quiet conversations. She often woke with a pit in her stomach on those unfortunate weekend days.

Few were lucky, they were ordered to other stations. Most simply packed up their belongings and left town. Others spit and cursed at Riley and Ferris. They'd rant aloud until making a beeline for the saloon to drown their sorrows and gamble away what was left of their earnings.

A remainder were downright nasty, including a Mr. Riordan, who was fired an hour earlier.

"This fucking place can rot." Riordan's threats echoed off the rail cars under repair. "Except for that secretary. I wanna lie down with that bitch." Rumbles from other dejected men added to the cacophony outside.

"I'll get Riley." Ferris stood as a bottle shattered against the outside of the office door.

Kate shuddered.

"That's enough, go on now. The sheriff doesn't want to shoot you. Scat!" Riley's tone overcame the motley crew outside. "Go on."

As the men left, Riley kicked aside the broken glass and opened the office door. He cut an impressive figure in the setting sun, his shadow filling the doorway until the men left.

"Well, that went poorly." Riley came inside. "Kate, you alright?"

"She's fine. I was just about to call for you." Ferris snapped before she answered. "Thank you, Riley."

"You can thank me when all this bull shit is over. We're already getting lean on staff. Those men weren't the best. But the other two? They had families."

"I'm doing the best I can, Riley." Ferris peered over his spectacles. He respected the foreman, but even he didn't know how many could be retained.

"Alright then, I suggest we leave together. No late nights." Riley snorted.

"That would be wise." Ferris packed up his case as Kate collected her satchel. "Let's go."

Riley held the door as they passed through. Night was falling on Iris. It was time to get on home.

The town felt the impact of the firings. At the railroad's peak growth, three hundred men were working in the yards in Iris. Their number diminished week after week for several months.

The hotels and flop houses didn't have enough patrons. They faltered and closed. The owner of the general store sold his interests to an investor from out of town and they'd sent in a polite man to run it. He took over care of the post as well. The mail dropped off so radically, that the postal service decided to close its building.

Groups of ranchers and farmers quit. Most sold off parcels of land bit by bit in an attempt to salvage their deeds. Whole tracts of property and equipment went up on the auction block as the bank began foreclosing on those who could not pay. An air of discontent had existed in Iris for years. It made its way into town like a weed with persistent roots that kept burrowing into the hard ground.

The tension in the rail office wasn't as bad on other days of the week. Ferris and Kate kept it tidy. The railroad assured them that Iris was utilized. Still, Kate felt a lingering uneasiness. Sleepless nights were followed by nerve-wracking days. Kate was well over thirty now but still lacked a desire to go home.

Where is my real home anyway?

Her moments spent with Riley out in the yards were less chipper, for he began to speak of the workers' fears.

"These men don't know what to do. No savings. Mouths to feed. Don't say this to Ferris. I've given the rowdier ones my pay to get them to vacate. Extra cash stops the griping. Others are complaining that they're being bought off. They're proud men, Kate."

"You're doing your best." Kate soothed her mentor.

"They're making threats, not to just me, but you and Ferris. Tell me that you'll watch your back. Keep your gun loaded. Bring your whip." All the terminated ones eventually left, but not without adding grey hairs to Riley's head and beard.

"I will," Kate promised. "I'm gonna git out on horseback, see you Monday."

Kate began to head out on longer rides with Sonny to deal with the anxiety, often stopping to relax near the church and the stream that fed the town. Her mind would wander off into the rustling waters.

On such a day, Kate found solace in the gifts of strength and wisdom from Iris's lesser inhabitants. Kate dismounted and sat on a cushion of moss just outside of the water.

"Hello, Kate!" Ming.

"Oh, hello." Kate jolted to her senses at the creek bed.

"Ah Miss Kate, you take a long ride today?" Ming queried in her broken English.

"Yes, I did." Kate made an effort to appear cheery, but the Asian woman recognized Kate's melancholy from afar. Kate had always been kind, but Ming felt her increasing sadness each time she'd collected laundry.

"It's hard now, yes? Not the same." Ming sat down next to one of her few friends. She knew everything about Kate, even more than Riley or Ferris. "You think, yes? It is hard here, you strong Kate. But you need help."

Kate gazed quizzically at her friend. "What do you mean?"

"You English, so soft. Even in man's clothes." Ming twittered as she stood. "Come, Chin show you." The Oriental woman moved along the creek bed and motioned for Kate to follow.

As they enclosed in on Ming and Chin's encampment, Ming approached her husband, chattering in a lively voice. A curious Chin peered over her shoulder at Kate. He shook his head for a moment and returned to the conversation in harsh Chinese. Ming touched his shoulder with a chiding whisper. Chin shrugged and turned to Kate.

"Miss Kate, I have to show you. Today, no time to waste." Chin rushed into their tent and returned with a dark leather satchel. "Come, down this way."

Kate was perplexed. She'd been to their camp before, even divulged her secrets to them, but had never seen Chin act that urgently.

With a tug of her hand, Chin led Kate across a shallow part of the creek, away from his home. They hiked up a narrow swath of earth eroded from its surrounding shrubbery. Once over the top of the creek bluff, he led her around the back side of a mini grove to where the trunk of a tree was covered in an old burlap blanket.

Chin let go of Kate and looked her squarely in the eye.

"Miss Kate, you special. You different. Your kind may say blessed. I see you ready to learn. A secret. You give word today, you tell no one?"

"Yes." Kate trembled. She'd never seen this abrupt behavior from him before. "I give you my word, Chin. I will not tell," Kate replied in the most serious voice she could muster.

"Very well." The Asian man before her was suddenly full of an omniscient power. She felt majestic energy around them. Her skin warmed and tingled.

"I show you this once only, never again. You learn, practice later. Ancient art." Chin's face turned to sadness. "I, Ming, no children. We get old but wise." His words were laced with sadness from a heavy heart. "I share with you." Chin deftly walked to the covered tree and took the sack covering off.

The tree was marked with dozens of slight holes as if insects took curious bites from the plant. Chin produced shiny diamond-shaped pieces of metal from the burlap. "Shuriken," Chin whispered as he held out the objects for Kate to see. "The English call Moon Stars. They from Japanese assassins. I tell you, just watch now." Chin kept a piece in hand, set the sack down gingerly, stepped away from Kate, and turned towards the tree.

He pinched the star between his thumb and index finger and drew the piece to his ear. With succinct motion, Chin whipped his arm straight forward. Kate heard the faintest whir of the star flying past. The Shuriken hit the tree with a tap. Kate's mouth was agape at the sudden speed and fury of such a small weapon.

Chin tapped her shoulder. "Again. See," he commanded as he removed another star from the pouch. He flicked the metal into the tree with a swift swing. Before Kate asked how he did it, Chin proffered a third star and placed it in her hand. "Now you do."

He molded her fingers and guided her arm. "Do slow," he ordered.

The outside world seemed to fall away as Kate held the cold metal in her hand.

"Now fast!" he whispered.

Kate drew back, then sent the star flying higher up the tree from Chin's planted stars.

"Good but can be better. Lower aim." Chin's eyes sparkled as he plucked the weapons from the tree. "Again. Point finger to tree."

"Okay. I've got it." Kate fired the three stars in perfect order into the beaten plant.

"Good, good." Chin recovered the sharp objects from the tree he had long used for target practice in secret. He stopped to hold Kate's hand over his. "Miss Kate, I cannot give you Shuriken. But..."

In the setting sun, Chin grasped a quill, ink, and paper from his satchel. He set the moon stars on paper down in the dirt, traced over it with the quill, and blew on the page to dry the ink. Chin swiftly rolled up the tracing, tied it with a piece of burlap, and set it aside with the satchel. "You will keep, you can do this, yes?"

"Yes," Kate promised.

"Now, I teach you this. Open hand." Chin demanded of Kate as he gathered her right-hand palm up into his. He curled her fingers in and tucked her thumb on the outside. "Good fist. See?"

"Yep." Kate smiled.

Chin then pulled her thumb in such a way that it stuck straight out away from her palm. "Bad, see?"

"Yes. Don't stick my thumb out."

"Watch." Chin then inserted her thumb under Kate's curled digits. "Bad, bad. Break thumb." He then adjusted Kate's thumb back to the first position. "Now you do, both hands." Chin tugged both of Kate's hands forward. His sense of urgency flowed through her body. Kate correctly drew fists. "Yes, yes!" Chin chirped excitedly.

"Now turn to jaw." Chin pushed Kate's tightened hands to her chin. "Turn and push like this." He straightened Kate's arm.

"Are you teaching me to punch?" Kate asked in amazement.

Brawling is for silly fools. This is far from a ladylike activity. But then again, she had come a long way from fancy satin gowns and formal high teas.

"Shhhh. Yes, quiet, now do. One hand, then other. Stand solid, like on horse, feet apart." Kate did as Chin directed, drew her fists in, and then punched the air with her right hand. "Again," Chin barked. Kate complied and switched arms. "Again," Chin ordered. He smiled in admiration for a moment, then his expression fell as Kate shadow boxed.

"Am I not doing it right?" Kate grimaced.

"Yes, right Miss Kate." Chin came close to her and put his hands over hers. "So little time left, Kate. You do it on your own now. Do not ever forget. You are strong." Chin's brown eyes peered deep into Kate's. "Come, we eat, rest, talk."

Soon they were relaxing in the tent. The flames from the campfire flickered around a pot filled with boiling soup. Ming ladled out generous portions of the steaming sustenance for each of them. Chin chanted a blessing in Chinese and he motioned at Kate to commence eating. The greens and spices in the meal filled Kate with warmth and satisfaction.

They sat on plush pillows under a blanket of fine Texas stars. In the dancing firelight, Kate noticed how happy Ming and Chin were. They didn't have material goods, yet together they radiated a joy she'd not witnessed among other couples in Iris.

After the meal, Chin pulled out a long, engraved ebony pipe, packed it with fragrant, dried leaves, and began to partake of its embers. He passed it to Ming. After a deep inhale, she in turn handed it to Kate and spoke. "Slowly. I have story for you."

Kate placed the pipe to her lips, drew in the smoke, and coughed.

"Try more." Ming encouraged.

On the second breath, Kate took a full draw. Her eyes closed briefly as her mind opened.

Ming's voice seemed to drift freely in the air as she began to speak. Gone was her meekness. Ming's tone evolved to a strength Kate never heard before.

"A long time ago, over a hundred years, my father born in China. From young age, his parents see he tall and strong. When he a man, The Emperor have soldiers make him be Shi. He became a great warrior."

As Ming spoke of her father, Kate envisioned his brilliant armor and the gilded images of the royal palace with the Emperor intact.

"After long battles, the Emperor ask him to guard the palace. Ninjas came to kill our king, but my father, he not let them. He caught their Moon Stars. He slay enemy. He brave, was given a lady, she was my mother. I live like princess. One day, a scribe, he come write history king's dynasty." Ming paused a moment and motioned to Chin.

Kate felt the love between them like a rush of warm wind in the tent.

"I meet Chin each day for year, but Emperor did not like, he discover Chin have some Japanese family and banish him. Mother see we in love and ask father for escape. Once we go, we never go back. Father not give his sword or shield. He give Chin the Moon Stars to protect us."

Images of their travels to America became clear. Kate's mind filled with ships dancing on the ocean and long wagon rides.

"We come here, be married. Work is hard, but we share, have each other."

All went dark. A hand on her shoulder startled Kate to wake. She was flat on her back on a blanket. Her eyes opened to Ming's smile.

"Tea Miss Kate?" Ming passed a cup to her friend.

"Hmm." Kate sat up and sipped at the warm liquid.

Did I dream this?

"You sleep well. You hard worker." Ming touched her shoulder.

Chin chimed in. "Remember, you strong Kate."

"Thank you." Kate quenched her thirst by downing the rest of the soothing tea. "I should sleep."

"Yes, yes, come." He aided a weary Kate off the blanket. "Drink water, rest."

The ground seemed to float below Kate as they walked to Sonny.

Wow, that was a dream. I will practice this.

"A wise man said, 'wherever you go, go with your heart.' Stay kind Miss Kate but be ready for change. Goodnight."

"Goodnight." A cool breeze cleared Kate's mind on the ride home.

When she emptied her riding satchel as she prepared for bed that night, she unrolled Chin's tracing and recognized that the Moon Stars appeared to be like the gears of a clock.

Kate trusted the couple. After all, they were privy to her secrets.

1879

Dear Papa:

I have been remiss in not writing sooner. The railroad continues to cut staff here. My employment is secure for now but please don't fret, I've enclosed my usual amount of funds. I hope it is going far to help.

I miss you and my dear sister, Abby. I know that it has been such a long time since I left, but I hope to return soon. God bless you all.

With all my love,

Kate

"What is that?" Kate was jolted from her papers and was ready to go home.

It had been a long, hot day about five years after Kate's arrival in Iris. The railroad was booming, which meant lots of sweaty, dirty men, and filthy clothes and rags. Ming and Chin had already wheeled two carts full of laundry to the creek when their donkey had enough. He brayed, bucked, and bit at Chin. He didn't budge and the cart was filled with a third load. It was Chin's retort in Chinese to the exhausted burro that jarred Kate.

"What's going on out here?" she peered out to overhear Chin swearing at the beast outside the rail office.

Ming came forward. "The donkey, he tired, he no go today. Too hot for him."

"Oh no." Kate moaned. The office would be closing, and they needed clothing and rags for clean-up tomorrow. Kate's eyes lighted with an idea. "Wait here," she implored Ming and ran to the general store.

Within ten minutes, a breathless Kate returned to the unhappy creature. "Here, I have sweets, water, and an apple."

The donkey dug into the nourishment with gusto. Bits of food that made it past his lips were licked straight off the desert floor. Kate drew her fingers away to prevent them from getting eaten. The beast brayed with joy when finished and rambled off to the creek without its owners.

"I get him." Chin laughed and ran after. Just then, the five o'clock train whistle blew.

"Well, that should do it." Kate nodded satisfactorily at her wash woman. But Ming seemed crushed, dark rings under her eyes revealing her lack of sleep.

Ming smoothed the hair from her cheeks as if she could barely lift the sweaty strands. "Ming, what's wrong?"

"So much work, so tired." Ming sighed sadly. Her body was defeated from the heat, coated with sweat and dirt.

Kate tugged another apple and sweets from her pocket. "Ming, eat this. It'll make you feel better," she urged.

"No hungry, lotta laundry," she mumbled and retreated with Chin to the creek, her head down and arms folded.

"Ming, Ming, what's wrong?" Kate locked the office door and caught up with Ming. Kate touched her shoulder, but Ming continued to walk, her face buried in her hands and weeping.

Ming's dress required cleaning. "Ming, stop, please. Tell me what's wrong." Kate had never seen her so sullen.

"It's hard. Too hard. So much, too much." Ming sobbed and turned an embarrassed red.

"Ming, I'm sorry. I can help. Wait here." Kate hustled to the tool shed behind the office. She returned with a contraption for Ming and Chin. "See, I've made you a better wash board. And here, you turn the crank at the top and press the clothes through the rollers to dry them."

"Oh," was all Ming managed to say. She touched the machine as if it'd appeared out of thin air. She and Chin were outsiders and desired little company or possessions.

"Well, let's not just stand here. Let's try it out." Kate grabbed her hand and they skipped to the creek. Chin unloaded the cart onto the creek bank. The donkey was happily tied to a tree and eating wet grasses. Huge piles of smelly clothes seemed to cover the creek line. "Whoa, my goodness." Kate gasped, then realized why Ming was despondent. "Okay, well then, let's begin."

"No, Kate, no." Ming pouted. "Board is enough."

"Don't be stubborn." Kate pulled off her boots and rolled up her sleeves. She tilted the washboard against a sturdy rock. "Where's the soap?"

Ming handed her a waxy lump and the three of them cleaned the massive washing in the late afternoon sun. Ming and Kate rubbed, rinsed, and wrung while Chin hung the clothes to dry on long ropes tied to trees lining the creek bed. As they finished, Chin jumped fully clothed into the creek, rinsed off, whispered to Ming, and headed to their tent around the bend of the creek. "Chin prepare dinner, okay?"

"Oh yes, I am famished," a weary Kate groaned. "And filthy," she moaned as Ming hung the last shirt on a line.

"We clean now." Ming chirped. And without another word, Ming untied the lacings on her dress and dipped naked into the cool spring-fed waters.

Kate's mouth fell open.

"Come, wash!" Ming laughed.

Kate checked around nervously, then unbuttoned her shirt and trousers. It had been years since she'd skinny-dipped with others around, and it brought back memories. Events that soon became apparent to Ming too.

Kate undid her corset and bloomers and slid into the water. It was blissfully refreshing on her body.

"See good!" Ming laughed.

Yes, yes, good.

Ming handed her soap and they cleaned. Kate dipped her head back in the water and smoothed her hair as she came up the bank, standing waist-high in the water. She slopped her wet mass of long hair to the side, preparing to pile it on her head when a cry from Ming startled her.

Ming pointed directly at her, yammering in Chinese.

Kate panicked. *Was it a snake? A coyote? Cowboys? Indians?*

Ming rushed to her side and touched her back while chattering in Chinese.

Oh no...the whip marks, Kate remembered sadly.

"Hurt? It hurt?" Ming stuttered.

Kate flushed with embarrassment. "No, no, Ming. It's okay, it happened a long time ago."

Ming's brown eyes filled with tears of sympathy. She caressed the flesh scarred from whipping.

"We go, we eat, we make better. Come." Ming led her to the clothesline, took off a long shirt, dry trousers, and assisted in dressing Kate. "Go to tent now, okay?"

Kate smelled a deliciously fragrant aroma as they rounded the corner to their home. Ming hurried ahead and whispered to Chin. In a stunned fashion, he took her hand and led her inside.

"Sit, sit," he urged. The well-built tent was high enough to stand in, with glorious pillows and covers inside, including a secret stash of linens they brought long ago from China. They made a tent out of heavy woolen sheets over a sturdy wooden frame. Oil lamps and several chests surrounded the walls. Chin guided her to the floor and went outside to tend to the fire that was boiling their dinner in an iron black kettle.

"We better now?" Ming smothered her with attention and stacked pillows together into an inviting pile. "Lay here, shirt off. On belly, yes? Okay?"

"Yes, okay." Kate surrendered.

Kate turned her back to Chin and took the shirt off. She didn't know which side of her body she was more embarrassed about. As she went belly down onto the scented exotic pillows, she heard Ming open the chests and the clinking of bottles. Kate peeked up to see her pull a cork out of a colored glass container.

"Okay, rest now," Ming instructed, and Kate closed her eyes as a unique scent enveloped the tent. "Tea tree oil, for skin." Ming soothed as she rubbed a smooth liquid over the seven lashes that penetrated Kate's tender back.

She moaned contentedly. Her back hadn't been touched since the day before she'd left St. Louis when she'd left home. Kate felt the sting of tears come to her eyes as she remembered a painful incident and hid her emotions. But it was too late.

Ming felt Kate's halted breath through her back. "You tell me," Ming whispered in her tiny voice. "Our secret, okay?"

As if hypnotized, Kate revealed the best and worst day of her life.

Ming listened as she massaged, then applied several scented, hot needles into select pressure points of Kate's back.

For the first time in years, Kate embraced clarity; she revealed what happened. Her body relaxed with relief from the ancient art of acupuncture.

Sharp pokes at the end of the scars near Kate's right hip rattled her awake. "Ouch!"

Ming soothed in her ear, "I mark you, for protection. The sign for strong. Keep evil spirits away. Cover part of hurt." She held up a mirror where Kate saw a tattoo covering the former curl of a whip mark.

"Wow," Kate admired the work. She was strong indeed and she called upon those emotional reserves over and over.

"We eat." Chin brought heaping plates of noodles mixed with chunks of savory meats and vegetables to the ladies.

The threesome ate as a rainbow halo circled a rising full moon outside.

"Ring around the moon, rain soon," Chin commented in a sullen mumble. "Rain to come here. Be careful, Kate."

Kate gulped as she put her plate aside. Chin was talking about more than just the weather.

"Here, gift, to soften pain," Ming lightened the mood as she handed Kate a silken dressing gown. "Go home, rest."

The gown provided more comfort than Ming would've ever guessed.

4 SHOOTOUT

Iris, Texas – 1894

"Deal." Kate scanned over her hand. She was ready to win after a long week in the rail yard. Her life in Iris was a steady rhythm of tasks, gambling, and rides on Sonny. She'd become proficient enough in her weaponry that Riley felt secure in introducing her to the local poker games.

"I'm in." Riley absently counted his chips. He and Kate began socializing with Ferris and friendly employees, often playing cards in the saloon after work for the distraction. Riley couldn't keep Kate away from the town's seedier side forever.

"Drinks?" The new saloon owner Miss Ellie sashayed along the room filled with eager players. The former dancer from Kansas ran the only real entertainment in town: drinks, saloon girls, and a Saturday night poker game that drew workers, travelers, ranchers, farm hands, and cowboys. Cards and chips flicked across the tables as games progressed.

"Two pair." Kate gathered her winnings without fanfare. With Riley's guidance, she played with ease and discretion that often upended her competition. "Sending some of this back home." She whispered to Riley as the next round was dealt. A short few weeks after Kate's thirty-fifth birthday, these games became a necessity; her employment was in question. The railroad was moving on, taking most of Iris with it.

"Wise. Save it for a trip home." Riley took his new hand from the dealer with renewed focus. The rail yard was near empty save a couple of old boxcars. He, Kate, and Ferris were the only rail folk left. Trains stayed only for the most urgent of repairs. Less than fifty remained in Iris and that included the manager of the general store, a sole surviving hotel, the orphans' home, and the saloon.

"What if I don't go back?" Kate bantered whilst examining her cards.

"You know you can't stay here. Some of us have to." Riley waved towards the window as Ming and Chin walked by outside. They were too old to leave. No one was willing to hire elderly foreign folk when plenty of young travelers were readily available. The couple now made their living by cleaning at the hotel and saloon. Kate aided them with the heavier laundry.

They shouldn't be working at all, she glanced out the window. *These kids shouldn't be here either.* Sister Theresa attended to a handful of children outside the general store. Their playful laughter carried over the clatter of games at the saloon. The young nun remained faithful to the orphans left.

"It'd be nice if we could keep a sheriff here." Kate grimaced as the distraction cost her a game. Lawmen came and went or were killed.

"We're fighting a losing battle." Riley tossed in a decent amount of chips. "Hell, the priest doesn't even live in town, comes in on a carriage once a week to do funerals and Mass. Same for the doc. The rail assigned him to a prosperous town further down the line. He'll drop in if we wire an emergency. But how often has he been too late? I mean, the undertaker is still in business, although he's not always fairly compensated for this increasing violence.

And regular gunfights in the street." Riley griped as he lost another hand.

"I know, I know." Kate bemoaned a wasted round. She sensed the developing fear in the town. Most went about their business but held out hope that a prospector might buy out their interests. A lot of property and land exchanged hands, but the once-booming town was dying.

"Whelp, it's time to go. It's getting dark." Riley spoke in code. Thieves tended to ride into town at sunset. Occasionally a body was found on the edge of town. Rumors flew that they'd have a cattle brand mark on them—a triangle with a "D" inside.

"Yep," Kate cashed in her chips. "You know I'm not attending any scoundrel's funeral." She wasn't the only one.

Few townsfolk showed up to mourn, including a Widow who'd arrived about five years earlier—a quiet woman who always wore a black dress and layers of veils. These unfortunate events had previously given the town a brief chance to connect, but many tired of the increasing deaths and stayed away.

Kate didn't like funerals. In fact, it was she who put a couple of those men in the ground and not by choice.

"Night, Kate." Riley crossed the street as the distant thunder of arriving horses rolled.

"Goodnight." Kate climbed up to her room. She didn't like violence or how rough Iris had become, but when coerced, Kate protected the weak. Tonight, she didn't feel like being pushed into any scuffles. "They can go to hell." Kate huffed as she fell asleep.

1890

Kate's first intervention happened about halfway through a Saturday night poker game. The saloon was crowded with most of the town seeking entertainment and refuge from a raging thunderstorm outside. A successful cattle drive brought in temporary residents. It seemed like prosperity had returned to Iris. The room was thick with cigar smoke and the smell of whisky. The dance hall girls kicked and twirled their vibrant costumes to the pianist's upbeat planking on the keys. Ellie was serving drinks as fast as possible.

"You seem to be doing well." Ferris stopped by, although to check on Kate rather than play. Her reputation as an astute competitor earned her a seat at a higher stakes berth.

"Yep." Stacks of chips from successful rounds of play were at her fingertips.

"Your good luck charm is working, I see." Ferris flirted. Strax sat at her feet as she played.

"Yes, now, I need you to be less charming." Kate chided without her eyes leaving the competition.

"Let her play," Riley whispered as he pulled himself away from the neighboring game. Ferris dutifully observed with the rail foreman.

Sitting next to Kate was a recently arrived drifter, Slim, who hadn't won a single round. He became visibly agitated, tugging at his hat and curling his lip with each round. Slim grunted upon losing, then began swearing so loudly that the other competitors heard him above the din of the busy saloon.

Sensing the disruption, Strax whined at Kate's side. Others exchanged nervous glances.

"You all, give me watcha got, now!" Slim stammered at his final loss. The table rattled as he jumped to draw his gun.

The entire room froze. Strax's growl permeated the silence.

"Shut that vile beast up!" He pointed his pistol directly at Kate.

Strax barked in defense of his owner, the hairs on his back standing on end.

"Sir—" Kate pleaded, "please don't do this." She pushed Strax back down under. The crowd chimed in agreement.

The slight, brash character only grew angrier with people watching. "Naw, naw, give me it all, load up your winnings!" Townspeople ran and hid behind any possible shield. His free hand pushed a torrent of unkempt brown hair back into his hat to reveal narrow dark eyes that returned to Strax. "Shut him up!"

Strax repeatedly barked despite Slim's threatening anger.

Slim aimed at Kate, ready to fire. He hollered as he readied the trigger.

"Bitch!" was the final word Slim ever uttered. The poor soul never got the shot off. Kate's shot went straight through his temple. Slim slumped to the floor as the crowd cowered in fear.

Kate drew her gun so swiftly, that most didn't see it was she who took down the errant gambler. The bang roared through her ears. She shook as Riley grabbed her hand and pushed the gun into its thigh holster that was strapped to Kate's leg.

He tugged her petticoat down over the weapon. Being a woman worked to her advantage. Kate wore dresses when playing poker. Male players tended to underestimate a female. The gown also efficiently hid her gun.

Riley whispered as he turned her back to the game, "Relax Kate, don't stare, pretend as if nothing happened, okay?"

It was the first time she'd ever shot a person. Her limbs stiffened like brittle branches as she fell into shock. Riley assisted her back to her chair in a lady-like sitting position.

The undertaker stood and asked the gambler next to him, "Help me pick up that body."

"Alright now, it's over, keep playing on." Ellie rushed over with rags and a bucket. She motioned to the piano whose flamboyant player was hiding fearfully behind it. He hoisted himself back to the keys and the music began again. The dancers came from the other side of the stage curtain, high-stepping, with their bloomers peeking out to the reenergized crowd. It turned out that only Kate's companions saw who'd stopped Slim. No one wanted to be involved. It was eerie how the room returned to normal. Cards were dealt, hands won and lost.

But not for Kate. She was quivering. As the game resumed, her hands shook as she picked up her cards. She drained of color. Strax nudged at her leg to console her in a way that only animals knew how. The room seemed to spin in slow motion as Kate realized she'd just killed a man.

Did I just shoot him? I did. What have I done? Why are we still playing poker?

The current round was over. An attractive regular at the saloon, Mr. Whitney, won.

Riley saw an opportunity to leave and leaned into Ferris, "Escort her home now. I'll stay here." Ferris agreed. There had been enough disturbances in the game, and they avoided drawing any attention.

"Alright boys, we're out," Ferris announced as he took Kate's hand and escorted her away. Strax shook and scratched himself, ready to go home with his master.

The gamblers snickered, believing Ferris was going to get lucky with Kate. Mr. Whitney snorted with jealousy.

They walked out of the saloon without incident and into a night cooled by the storm that passed. Strax trotted along, his paws getting muddy in the muck of the street.

"Kate, are you okay?" Ferris leaned in protectively.

"Yes, yes, I'm alright. I did what I should," Kate reasoned aloud. "He could've killed me." The chill outside awoke her senses and she shivered.

"Yes, indeed. Kate, how did you learn to draw like that? Most impressive!" Ferris beamed.

"Riley taught me. Now don't go bragging like that," she rebuked, "This town is gettin' smaller every day and you know it's become dangerous." They stopped outside the saloon. Strax ran up to the top, waiting to go inside their humble room. "Don't say anything, pretend like nothing happened, you understand?"

"Of course." Ferris agreed but he desperately desired to kiss her goodnight.

Alas, Kate collected herself without romantic notions. "Alright then. Now go home and be careful."

"I will Kate." He kissed her hand. A disappointed Ferris blended into the darkness as she went upstairs.

Strax plopped on the floor next to the bed and rested his head on his paws. Kate undressed and sat on the bed. Only then did she bury her sobs into her pillow to prevent her from being heard.

A week later, Kate went to Mass and Confession when the priest came to town. Behind the curtain of the confessional, the holy man wondered to himself, *how did a place get so violent that women were now doing the shooting?*

Although no one saw her draw her pistol, several remembered that it was Kate who was the first to challenge Slim. Talk of it floated at his burial. Kate didn't dare attend the funeral of a man she'd shot.

The Widow came in late, but she'd overheard the gossip from attendees that maybe, just maybe, justice was coming back to Iris.

From that day on, as the town's pitiful situation grew worse, they turned to Kate or Mr. Riley when trouble commenced.

July 1895

"That gang of cowboys has been coming to town each day." Riley packed up for the night.

"It doesn't help that the new sheriff told them that they could settle their disputes with a duel on the noon train whistle. What a fool he is for firing up trouble." Kate slipped her satchel over her shoulder. The town was eroding.

Folks were getting testy; fights were breaking out over the smallest infractions in the saloon. Even the weekly Saturday night poker game was getting testy. Most were transients that played to pull in extra cash before the train's next stop. They replaced most of the regulars who'd come to quench their thirst after a long day of ranching.

Ellie hired men to keep order, but none stayed for long. They either were threatened, paid to leave, or ended up joining the gang rumored to be led by a fella named Drasco. Only Ming and Chin were willing to stay. They made cash by assisting Ellie with cleaning. Kate sporadically did repairs. But they were no match for this deviant bunch.

"The infighting is terrible. How they stick together is a miracle." Ferris chimed in. "Headed for the saloon?"

"Naw, I'm tapped out. No poker for me." Riley pulled on his cap and stole a glance at Kate.

"Kate? You playing?" Ferris slipped on his jacket.

"Uh, no. I'm taking Sonny for a ride; I'll see you tomorrow." Kate pretended to gather papers as the five o'clock train whistle screeched.

"Goodnight then." Riley shuffled off. He harbored wishful thoughts that Kate would dress up and play as he still yearned for her.

Kate and Riley waited inside the office until Ferris was well out of earshot.

"He's still sweet on you, you know?" Riley teased. "It's not too late to run off into the sunset with him."

"Oh, stop." Kate groaned.

"Okay, seriously though. You know the rail might keep him, transfer him out. You could go—"

"I said stop. Besides, this isn't what you wanted to tell me." Kate chided.

"Right. Well, there's a duel tomorrow. I overheard talk at the latrine."

"What else is new?"

"It's the sheriff. He's in it."

"What? How?" Kate exclaimed.

"Seems his policy backfired on him. He caught a member of the gang stealing grain from the back of the general store. The cowboy disputed that claim, saying he was just moving the sack. So, the bastard asked him to settle it at noon."

"Shit. What do we do?" Anxiety crept into Kate's voice. "I'm making a repair for Miss Ellie tomorrow."

"We'll be there. They'll know about it by morning anyway. Just be prepared and know that we won't have a sheriff tomorrow afternoon." Riley noticed that Kate paled. "And try not to worry too much."

Riley was correct in his assumption. The next day the thief sent the unwise sheriff to an early grave. Onlookers to the tragedy included most of the town. Kate, Ferris, and Riley stood at the doorway of the saloon to watch.

The whistle blew. The sheriff didn't even get his hand to his holster. The thief snorted, holstered his gun, and mounted his horse without a word.

"Dang." Riley shook his head. "Fool."

The thief rode off as if it were a daily occurrence to shoot a lawman. But then he abruptly paused at the end of the main street to watch the crowd for a moment.

Several of the townsfolk looked to the remaining rail trio and an older townsman shouted, "Are you gonna do anything?" The crowd was desperate for a savior.

Riley spoke wisely, "You all go on about your business; this one's over."

Ferris chimed in, "Yes folks, go on now. I'll wire the rail about sending another sheriff."

The killing cowpoke overheard the chatter, turned his horse, and rode in front of the group. "Ha, this town don't have no sheriff, no law, no nothing. You all gotta leave." He cackled, drunk on bravado. "We own this town. Get out while you can 'cause we're gonna do whatever we want, see?"

Without warning, he blasted the older townsman that had come forward. The man's wife shrieked when he fell and dragged her down with him as blood gushed from his chest. The crowd took cover, including Ferris who pushed the townswomen inside the saloon. Riley attempted to stop the oozing vermillion flow from the poor soul who was dying out in the open.

Just as the gunman was prepared to ride off, another bang was heard and screams added to the din. This time it was the thief that was hit, flat in the forehead and he slumped forward on his horse. The beast was startled by the gunfire and galloped away with its dead rider still hooked in the stirrups.

Kate's eyes never left the shooter after his show down with the sheriff. He'd been cocky that morning of the duel, after the verbal scuffle over the stolen grain sack with the lawman. He bragged loudly to anybody who'd listen in the saloon about how he was taking down the only law in town. He was sorely mistaken; Kate overheard his tirade as she'd repaired a door in the saloon for Miss Ellie. Her anger grew with his boasting.

Be especially wary of this one, she cautioned herself.

Kate's hand had been at her hip from the moment the competitors strode into the street. When the brazen fool grabbed for his gun, she got a clean shot. As the sounds of the horse galloping away quieted and the smoke cleared, Riley sadly glanced at Kate. He was morose that her life was forever changed. Kate would be relied upon. Not as a sheriff, but she'd decided to no longer stand idly by.

Kate turned to the stooped crowd; her gun already holstered. "Is everybody alright?" she asked, shocked at her clarity.

The townspeople dusted off, stunned by the shootout. Quiet words followed and the undertaker jumped in as the older man died.

Riley stood and wiped his shaking hands. He was getting too old for this life.

Ferris assisted the newly widowed woman along as she wailed painfully. As he ushered her behind the wagon that carried her departed, he anxiously stared back at Kate.

She spoke in a serene tone, "Alright now, Mr. Tomley will be wiring for a new sheriff. Go on home." The crowd dispersed, more enthused than just a few minutes before.

Riley began to speak, but Kate stopped him. "I know, I know. I just stepped into the biggest pile of horse shit."

That Sunday another funeral commenced. The older man was buried. Having seen what happened, most of the town attended, including the Widow.

Kate arrived after the service and unburdened her conscience to the visiting reverend. The town was quiet, but not for long.

Three weeks later… August 1895

"A vagrant just threatened the girls in the Saloon." Ferris rushed to Riley in the rail yard. "We should get over there."

"Yep. Let's go." Riley threw down his tools and collected his guns. Another sheriff died mysteriously since the last lawman was shot in the duel. Iris was going downhill fast.

Across town, residents were either sleeping off a hangover or doing productive work. No one in the saloon was available to keep this passer-through in check.

"Come here, missy." He got touchy-feely with the dancers. He was a hairy beast of a man, burly with a rotting hat and teeth. His eyes were red from copious amounts of alcohol and not enough sleep. His knotted hair dripped greasily down his back and his matching beard did the same down the front of his shirt. His clothing was filthy, covered in dust and mud from traveling. His meaty hands clawed at the girl.

"Hey, let go of her!" Ellie intervened. "Pay up and get on out of here."

"I ain't got no money." He shoved the dancer aside, pushed Ellie down, and pulled a gun.

It was at that moment that Kate came into the back of the bar for a drink after fixing the saloon's water pump in the rear.

The squeak of the bar doors distracted the interloper, and he drunkenly pointed his pistol at Kate as she entered. "Well now pretty lady, pour me a drink will ya?" he slurred.

Strax galloped in behind Kate, stopped at her side, and emitted a low growl.

Kate cleared her throat and gauged the situation. She was unarmed. Ellie struggled to pull herself up. A couple of dance hall girls were hovering towards the back of the stage, trapped in the dressing room.

"Sir, you've just hurt your bartender. If you wait a moment, she'll get your drink when she's able," Kate intoned with a sense of clarity.

"What? Bitch! Pour me a goddamned drink! You're fucking whores." He yammered towards the bar.

Kate saw her opportunity and flung a hefty mug at the fool's hand, knocking away his pistol. He stood dumbfounded that he was challenged. His hand bled as Ellie came around and crawled to the girls behind the stage. Strax barked, but Kate held him back.

She persuaded the errant vagrant to quiet. "Now then, there's no need for any violence, right?" Kate was rudely interrupted by the entrance of Mr. Drasco, a man of questionable nature.

Drasco stood in the doorway and leered at the fallen fool. "Well now mister, seems like you've gotten into a tussle with Miss Kate Church and her 'lil mutt, haven't you?" He smirked, calling out Kate by name on purpose. Kate hadn't been about town since the death of the townsman. She avoided drawing Drasco's ire.

Drasco was a roughhewn man with an even shadier reputation. He was in his late forties and battered from the elements. His unkempt beard was a squirrel's nest of brown and gray. The deep brown pools of his eyes appeared black as night under his ten-gallon. He'd been in town or a least passing through for five years, buying up the dry land and deserted properties. The abandoned farms and shacks he'd purchased remained mostly empty save a couple of buildings in town he used as warehouses for whatever contraband he was dealing. He commanded a similar well-worn crew of rowdy thieves under him.

The drunken cowboy drawled, "What you gonna do about it? Huh? You thinkin' I'm a sissy, lettin' my arse get whupped by a girl?"

"Oh no, sir. You might want to take these matters outside and save what pride you got left. You should challenge her to a duel, eh?" Drasco let out a deep gravelly belly laugh.

Kate stiffened and Strax whimpered, sensing his master's discomfort. She'd been waiting for the day that Drasco attempted to get rid of her, one of the brave that stood up to these rascals. Unfortunately, that moment arrived.

Drasco waved his meaty paws in Kate's direction. "Oh, she's tough, but I bet a bastard like you could hold her down." He laughed. "You know, we like a gunfight around here at noon, right when the train whistle blows as it leaves." Drasco eyed Kate to see if she was panicking.

Ellie was instantly anxious. Her heart pounded in her ears. Few were left to protect any of the girls if Kate was killed. She was certain her day to die wouldn't be far behind Kate's destruction.

But if Kate was nervous, it didn't show. *Breathe and stay calm.* Her voice was the purest example of reason, "Sir, we don't want any trouble around here; I can get you a drink and get you settled."

Drasco interrupted, "Aw no, this man isn't a fool, are you son? You let that lady make an ass out of you?" He egged him on, stirring up trouble. The room was full of tension. The saloon girls still cowered in the corner with Ellie standing in front of them. Residents heard the commotion and peered in the windows.

"Heck no," the fool exclaimed, "I'm ready now!"

"Well then," Drasco bellowed, "it'll be noon in about ten minutes. I say we have a gun fight then. What about it, Miss Church?" He laughed viciously.

"I guess we do then," Kate murmured. Drasco was salivating at the idea of being through with her.

"Well then, noon it is!" he exclaimed.

Riley and Ferris pushed through the growing crowd and followed Kate out the door along the porch of the saloon. Strax kept pace faithfully beside her. Riley caught her arm at the corner of the building.

"Miss Kate, you don't have to do this," Riley urged. "He's taking the town over. Let him have it. You don't have to die for it."

"I know, but if I don't, all hell will break loose. Let's get a plan together. I need to buy time," Kate spat. "Meet me in front of the saloon."

"Time for what?" Ferris inquired.

"Just get the town together to watch," she yelled as she ran up the stairs to her room, Strax followed eagerly behind. "I'm putting on a show they won't forget," Kate mumbled to herself as she pulled a simple case from under her bed. Inside was a unique gun and tubes. She fashioned a pistol small enough that it fit in the palm of her hand, with equally tiny bullets. Instead of gunpowder, embossed in the handle was a miniature globe of glass that held a peculiar, but powerful green liquid. All she'd have to do is raise her hand high enough to shoot; the magic liquid made even the fastest shooter appear slow. She steadied her hands around her secret weapon.

Kate found the mysterious liquid completely by accident. The stolen sack of grain that inadvertently killed a sheriff, was obstructing others like it. After that first duel, she went to return the sack the cowboy stole. But in his zest of temporary victory, he left it on the porch of the general store.

When Kate set the grain sack down behind the general store, a tube filled with green liquid rolled into the dirt. She felt into the bag and the grain concealed curious tubes capped with corks. Kate had never seen anything like it. The thief wasn't stealing it; he was indeed moving the stack when the now-deceased sheriff caught him. She gingerly searched the sacks in the pile. Each contained hidden tubes. Kate buried several in her satchel and assumed correctly that they wouldn't miss just a small number of them.

Kate got away from the town and into the desert to experiment a couple of days later. She found out the liquid was highly flammable and even explosive. She first held a tube up to the sun and then uncorked it. Kate took a deep whiff. It smelled fruity, but in a liquor-like fashion. Kate tripped and dropped a tube by accident. It hit a rock and exploded with a bang. An idea warmed her.

She poured out a trickle on another desert stone, hit it with flint, and it evaporated with the flame in a flash. It was highly volatile, but she figured only a nominal amount created a faster weapon. She poured the liquid into a bead she'd embedded in a gun handle. The trigger set off the liquid creating steam for a super-fast bullet. From that day on, Kate practiced with this unique weapon and kept it hidden under the bed for a special occasion. The kind folks in Iris were now outnumbered.

Kate slid the pistol into the holster at her hip, grabbed a hat, whipped on a set of welding goggles, and threw on her heavy leather coat. She was fully engaged in the present.

"You have to stay here," she cooed to Strax and tied his leash to the bed. She worried he'd run into the street when the shooting started. Her heart ached for the canine she loved. It was minutes before noon when Kate burst into the saloon.

Riley and Ferris were waiting, as were most of the town. "Kate, don't do this," Riley begged.

"It will be okay. Watch the crowd, and keep them out of the way," she barked in a confidence so firm that Riley believed she'd gone mad.

"Kate, if you do this, I will have to terminate your employment," Ferris warned as they burst onto the porch.

"You won't have to fire me. I'll quit or die." Kate smirked and then adjusted her hat and goggles.

Here I am again, defending a town that's dying. Why do I do this?

Kate remembered her arrival and how Iris changed since then. Her past flashed before her: growing up in St. Louis, leaving due to horrific circumstances, learning the rail trade, and becoming an independent, skilled woman when most ladies were forced under the thumb of less than kind men.

Moments for reminiscing on her life in the face of death were over. Kate stepped out into the heat and the middle of the dusty main street.

The cowpoke turned out with a slight arrogance. Drasco gave him a new pistol, a couple of pointers, and a shot of confidence in the form of whisky. In the distance, the familiar roar and hiss of the steam engine of the exiting train echoed.

The adversaries dueled each other in the street. The whistle shrilled as the train left the station. The duel was over in a flash, although unseen by most onlookers. Kate's pistol and its whiff of green combustion steam were hidden due to the heavy coat. She'd drawn in a flash, the special gun fired so fast, that the marauder didn't even get his hand to his hip. Kate hit him in the direct center of the chest, and he instantly dropped dead to the dirt. Her hidden gun plan worked as planned; it was already tucked safely back in her belt. She shook off the tremble in her hand. The crowd clapped and hollered until a heavier shot echoed along the street.

Kate spun and listened but didn't hear where it came from. Her hands flurried over her body, checking herself.

Okay, no pain, I'm not hit. Where did that come from?

She returned her attention to the crowd. Most collapsed to the ground, screaming at the explosion of a second shot, but Riley was leaning on a porch support, his hand to his chest. The stunned foreman removed his bloodied palm. He slid down the beam and fell to the porch of the saloon.

Kate completely forgot that she was standing out in the open and screamed. "Ferris, get him inside the saloon! Get outta here!" she yelled as people scattered like crows.

Ferris and Kate carried Riley into the saloon and onto a table. His body left a rich, fresh trail of blood behind them.

"Ellie, get water and towels!" Kate shouted, but it was too late. A dull roar ran through her brain.

Riley was coughing up trickles of vermilion. More gruesomely dripped off the edge of the table from his back. A bullet ripped a hole clean through his jacket, shirt, and body. Kate and Ferris tried in vain to stop the bleeding. He'd been shot with a weapon bigger than a pistol.

This whole gunfight was a setup, a distraction, Kate's mind spun in a panic. Her mouth dried completely, and her limbs flailed as she attempted to save her friend and control her bitterness.

Riley grabbed her hand, and slurred inaudibly, "Kate, you did right. You did right."

Kate cried, the pain causing her chest to heave. "No, no, I did this. I shouldn't have."

Riley coughed harder, struggling with his last breaths. "You did right. Get out. You can't save the town." His voice was a choked whisper. He pulled her close with his remaining strength. "He'll own the town, but don't let him win by killing you. Get out, don't...let..him....win. Promise.. me." His words came out in hesitant gasps.

"Okay, yes, I promise." Kate sobbed.

A hollow gurgling emitted from Riley as he expired. Ferris collapsed into a chair; his proper suit splattered with blood.

"No, no, no." Kate bawled over Riley's body, not quite believing her mentor perished.

Ellie put her hand on Kate's shoulder. "Let him go." Riley and Kate's bloody hands were grasped tightly, and Ellie pried them apart.

"Okay." Kate sniffled. She anxiously shook off the tension in her body. It was deathly quiet in the saloon. It had been only minutes since the shootout, but it seemed like hours.

From across the street, Drasco's familiar cackle trailed behind as he and his gang left. Kate walked to a saloon window and watched them leave. With trembling hands, she wiped her tears and the blood off her hands. Despite the shock and trauma that just played out, she resolutely whispered to herself, "I will not let him win. I promise, Riley. Drasco will not win."

5 THE WIDOW

No one remembered the exact day the Widow arrived in Iris, but after the violence escalated, resulting in fear and funerals, the townsfolk came to recognize a dark figure. It was a woman who came to mourn, no matter who was buried. She was always properly dressed for a funeral, rain or shine, hot or cold, in a black dress with a train. She wore an elegant lady's hat, embellished with a satin bow and several veils that were so thick that you didn't see her face. Long black gloves completed her ensemble and ensured that every inch of skin didn't see the sun.

The funeral routine was always the same. Just as the service was about to begin, she entered the church and sat in a pew about halfway back. She didn't participate, except to express brief condolences to the main family member present as the coffin was walked out on its final journey. The pall bearers lifted the departed onto a rickety trailer for the short ride on the path to the cemetery just a stone's throw away from the church. She and the other mourners followed.

Those present at the final resting place of the departed stood silently as the priest intoned spiritual comfort and the body was lowered into a dusty grave. The Widow gave a donation to the clergyman, saying only that she knew how it felt to lose family. She left with the others to town but didn't join them for supper at the hotel or drinks at the saloon. Those mourning were usually distracted and upset at the sudden death of a beloved, that they didn't notice the Widow had disappeared.

The funeral of the cowboy Kate killed wasn't any different. Riley had been buried the day before and out of respect for the foreman, the priest stayed in town an extra day so that the kind rail manager didn't have to be laid to rest on the same day as a despicable fool. A handful of Drasco's gang and a woman who was said to be the cowpoke's sister attended with the Widow. No sooner was the dead man in the ground, than the Widow left.

In stark contrast, most of the town came to the funeral for Riley, including Kate. She and Ferris sat in the front row, as he died without any family. Kate was still aghast at his death. Her eyes were red from bawling, and she grasped Ferris' hand as if she'd never let go. Her manager was ghostly white. He remained stoic for the last employee under his tutelage.

The church was showing wear like the rest of the town. The chipped paint broke off in bits and pieces in the blustery western winds. The floorboards creaked as the faithful trudged into morn for the departed.

It was packed tightly with mourners. Women and children wept openly. Kate struggled to hold back tears.

Riley would chastise me for crying.

But at the gravesite, her grieving refused to be held back anymore. Tears rolled freely down her cheeks as the undertaker and Ferris threw on the first layers of ceremonial dirt. Drasco and his gang stood off out in the distance watching with interest. Kate barely saw them out of the corner of her swollen eyes. She hated them and her heart hardened despite her kindness.

Ferris reserved the main hall in the only open hotel with Riley's remaining earnings for a funeral luncheon. The rail manager thought it proper to have a memorial other than just drinks at the saloon. Largely vacant for years, the hotel's owner was grateful to have the business. Ellie and the dancers volunteered to serve food and drinks. Several stood and spoke of Riley's kindness and generosity. He'd died penniless, as he'd given most of his wages to the near-empty children's home. He'd never spoke of where he'd come from, but he was always hospitable about where others were going. Townspeople took turns speaking kindly of Riley, including the orphanage's Sister Theresa, who mourned in gratitude over his donations to the children.

When it was Kate's moment to share a kind word, she spoke solemnly. "The Bible says do unto others as they should do unto you. I hope that we should care as Mr. Riley did for others. God rest his soul."

The priest nodded in agreement. Claps and a chorus of "Amens" filled the room.

Kate felt validation from the crowd. Relief spread over her body in subtle, warming waves.

A husky cough from the doorway interrupted the celebration of life. The crowd turned round in awkward silence.

Drasco and his men rudely poked their heads in. Drasco rasped, "Friends, let's raise a glass to our dear departed then!"

The attendees looked to Kate with tension etched across their faces. The air thickened with anxiety. Children were held closer. Men reached for their weapons.

Kate stared the criminal down. She got a decent picture of the man that was destroying her oasis. She made note of a golden key hanging from his bandana.

Why isn't that key on a ring or chain? How dare he come in like this?

She raised her glass, "A toast, to Mr. Riley then." Hate panged in Kate's chest.

"Here, here," chimed in Ferris and Strax barked approvingly. They prevented the leader of bandits, thieves, and murderers from having the last word. Drasco and his men walked out. A cacophony of glasses and kind words filled the room. Outside the sun set over a somber Iris. Ming and Chin began cleaning, the mourners left, and the town was deprived of one of its greatest assets to Kate's dismay.

A gaping, emotional hole was skewered into her by Drasco and his gang. Her hands were stiff from clenching her fists.

Sensing her sadness, Ferris walked Kate home afterward. An air of trouble followed them like a cloud, ready to burst with hail.

"Kate, we have serious business to discuss tomorrow," he whispered. He soothed the woman he'd come to cherish. Her strength had been cut by vicious souls that frightened him and the town. He was bitter that they dared to come to the funeral but felt powerless.

"Yes, tomorrow we must," she griped wearily. They were in a most precarious position.

Ferris kissed her hand. "Goodnight Kate." He double-checked his new pistol and holster. They had belonged to Mr. Riley. Ferris could use them.

"Goodnight Ferris." She and Strax went up the stairs. Once inside, Kate didn't even light a lamp. She undressed in the dark, began to weep, and lay awake until far into the night. Strax whimpered with her until she fell into a restless sleep.

The Widow hadn't attended Mr. Riley's funeral, she'd had other mournful business to attend to that day. But the church was full, and her absence wasn't of concern.

6 THE FIRST INVITATION

The weeks after Riley's demise were tense. An uneasy stillness filled the town. People came and went in a flurry. After all, moving targets were harder to hit.

Drasco and his gang hadn't been around, but the town, in fits of fear, wondered when they'd be back. There wasn't solid proof of who shot Riley, but most assumed it was Drasco or his gang.

The first day back in the rail office without Riley was emotionally painful for both Ferris and Kate. When she walked in with Strax, her constant canine companion sniffed and whimpered, searching for the railroad foreman.

A dejected Ferris peered over his spectacles from his papers. "Good morning, Kate. Come in, please."

"Good morning." Kate began calmly.

He crossed the room and interrupted her. He was white as a sheet and his shoulders stiff with tension.

"Kate, I know I said you'd be fired, but I did it in haste. Considering what has happened, please stay, at least for a while. I only threatened termination because I was afraid, I'd lose you, but we've lost Riley instead."

Ferris was anguished in such a manner that it bothered Kate. She stood frozen at her desk. A chill ran through her. She had never seen him so despondent.

"I have bad news," Ferris continued. "The railroad has wired that the town has become too dangerous. Beginning October first, they won't be here on a regular schedule. The train will pass through, but only for passengers and deliveries that have wired ahead through the post. They are abandoning this office and they will no longer require our services." Ferris exhaled deeply and put a comforting hand on Kate's shoulder.

Kate was shaking. "What? They can't possibly close here. This can't be." She figured it was bad, but now the town was losing the trains too. Strax morosely peeked up at his master.

"I know this is horrible. I'm sorry." He witnessed her devastation.

Kate choked back her sadness but cried when she'd believed no tears remained.

Ferris drew her close to him and she sobbed into his chest. He was pleasantly surprised at her breakdown. He'd admired her strength, but he reveled in her lady-like side.

Ferris stole looks at her. He'd seen her kindness with Strax and the orphaned children, but Kate never appeared frightened of the threats. She was different from any woman he'd ever known: the prissy socialites from back East, the sassy saloon girls, and the innocent young women that eyed him as a possible suitor before he'd come to Iris. He enjoyed her candor and wisdom. He tried in vain not to think about Kate in other ways. He was struck by her beauty, even wearing men's duds. The warmth of her body near him felt heavenly, even in their sad situation. He wished they were somewhere else, in a safer, genteel atmosphere.

Kate felt a strange sensibility in her embrace with Ferris and backed away. *I can't lead him astray with romantic notions.*

"Thank you, Ferris, for your kindness and assistance," she intoned with such clarity that she stunned herself. Kate appreciated Ferris, and although he was her junior in age, he was still her superior at the office, if only for a while longer. "I must learn to contain myself." Her tender voice quelled her own emotions. He proffered his handkerchief from his coat pocket for her, and she dabbed her eyes with it.

Ferris cleared his throat. Perhaps he'd been too forward. He stuttered, "Yes, um, well then we talk about what we should do." It was late August, and October was just a few short weeks away.

"Has the rail office offered you another position?" she inquired, certain that Ferris would find a job with his management skills. Kate was so consumed with grief she hadn't even cared about herself.

"No, neither you nor I will be allowed to stay. I may go back East. Better opportunities for a person like me." He shrugged. "But until then, we have a duty to serve the town for the rail and we'll still receive pay. It won't be easy without Riley."

"When is the new sheriff arriving?" she asked. She still held the kerchief tightly as she bit her lip.

"They won't send one, Kate. We're on our own." The specter of danger enveloped the room. "I don't know what we're doing here." His words were cryptic, and a sick feeling rattled her intestines.

Kate mustered her courage and remembered her promise to Riley. "We'll leave, but until then we must stay vigilant."

"Well, of course, it'll just be us here in the office, holed up for the remaining weeks. Let Drasco have it all and we'll just disappear on October first." He appeared confident. He wistfully dreamed that they'd leave together.

"No." Kate was defiant. She thumped her palms on her desk and pushed her chair back. "We are targets now, and not just us. The whole town: we'll have to be extremely careful. We don't know who shot Riley, whether it was Drasco's men or someone else in town." Kate's grief turned to preparedness. She flushed with rising anger. "We'll act as if nothing happened. Keep a regular schedule, and fix what we can. Then maybe we can get the town to leave as we do."

"And how will we be able to do that?" Ferris asked awkwardly. He toyed with spectacles, wiping and cleaning them before putting them back on. The fidgeting betrayed the anxiety he wished to hide.

"I don't know, but I'll think of something," she replied. He nearly heard the cogs of the plan spinning in her head. He was grateful that she managed to stay grounded.

"Alright then. Well, let's get as settled here as we can. Start packing." he asserted. They weren't certain how long it'd be before the residents got word from the rail about the change. They surmised it best to stay quiet and avoid a panic. They went about their business that day believing no one else was privy. They were wrong. Subversive forces in and outside the town were already creating mischief.

After the last train rolled out, Kate went to the saloon to fix a water pump that was busted yet again. Kate wanted that money from Ellie to get out of town.

"Everything is broken in this town," Kate mumbled to herself, reattaching the pump's handle. As a shadow appeared beside her and Strax yelped, Kate jumped up and was startled by an orphan child. It was a young Negro boy, Tobias. He'd been abandoned at the platform months earlier. An offspring of former slaves, his father died, and his mother could not afford to keep him on her way to employment in California for a wealthy gold prospector. She'd heard that this boom town took children. Tobias's mother was wrong about the prosperity of the town, but correct that a kind nun, Sister Teresa, stayed to rear the children left in the orphans' home. Tobias was a radiant robust child of about seven, with a cherub's cheeks and curious nature despite his rough past.

"Good day Missus Kate. The man at the post had a letter for you." He handed her a brown twine-wrapped envelope. It wasn't from home, and she immediately grew suspicious.

She knelt next to him, took the envelope, and put a hand on his shoulder. "Tobias, who gave this to you? You won't be in trouble, okay?" Kate assured the child.

"The postman in the general store, Missus Kate. He didn't say where it came from." He blushed.

"Okay then, thank you for your delivery." She handed him a coin from her trouser pocket. His eyes grew wide with the offering. "You earned this. Now run along, go get yourself a treat at the store."

"Yes ma'am!" he exclaimed happily and scampered off. The moment he turned the corner of the saloon, Kate checked around and backed into the shadow of the building. She remained hidden to open the mysterious piece of mail. She unwrapped the twine to find a folded letter of fine parchment, a hundred dollars in paper monies, and a card simply marked:

"Read in a private place, W."

The paper was sealed with red wax and imprinted with an elegant letter "W." She had not a clue who "W" was and who was wealthy enough to just give away money? Kate glanced over her surroundings, stuffed the loot in her pocket, and opened the letter. It read:

"Dear Miss Church:

I understand that you are seeking employment considering that rail service will come to an end in Iris. I am a businessman from an Eastern city who desires that several duties are handled in a most professional manner. These tasks are to be completed in a neat and covert fashion as I am wealthy and wish to remain anonymous. You have knowledge and expertise that would fulfill the duties.

In return for your service, I will pay you in cash for each. If you are willing, please return the enclosed card to the Post by 3 p.m. tomorrow. Simply hand it to the postman; he will know what to do with it. Act in a quiet accord and do not draw attention to yourself. You can pick up your other letters or packages, but a reminder, your confidence is of the utmost importance. I will send further instructions should I receive the card. If you are not interested in this proposition, please burn the enclosed card and this letter at your earliest convenience. I hope that you will heavily consider this opportunity; you will be well rewarded for your efforts. As a gesture of my sincerity, I have enclosed $100. Thank you for your consideration.

Your Benefactor,

W."

Kate again surveyed the surrounding area, completely flummoxed. Not a soul in sight. Strax cocked his head sideways as if he were perplexed as well. She tucked the letter and its wrappings into her satchel. She made the final adjustments to the water pump handle. Once fixed to her satisfaction, she scooped up her tools, filled a bucket, and entered through the back door of the saloon. All the while she stewed about the letter.

Was this a trap set by Drasco?

She didn't know if the villain was even literate. He had cash, but he didn't seem like the kind of man that'd simply drop a hundred dollars to draw her in when he could shoot her in the street. And cowboys weren't the type of men to buy fine parchment, let alone use an imprinted wax seal.

Additional money to get out of town.

Kate reasoned that perhaps she'd drop the card off at the post. Questions tumbled in her mind.

Was this real? How did this person know to find her?

Kate was both elated and anxious. As Kate set the bucket down in the back room of the saloon, she heard the familiar clicking of Ellie's boots as she approached. "It's fixed." Kate waved to the bucket full of water.

"Well, Amen to that," Ellie drawled in a pleasant southern accent. "Can't keep this place clean enough and I've got plenty of thirsty patrons in this heat. Although they usually don't want water." She laughed pleasantly. Ellie was a stunning southern belle whose family came west after the Civil War. Her long, wavy raven hair was in stark contrast to her pale skin and deep brown eyes. She often tucked her tresses up in a high twist and tied them with exotic plumes and ribbon. Her generous womanly figure was covered in vibrant satin dresses. Her beauty and a whip-smart attitude made the saloon popular. But her lifestyle of tending to a bar in a violent town was wearing on her spirit. Despite the enthusiasm of dwindling thirsty patrons, Ellie fussed she wouldn't keep it alive. Perhaps it was time to leave.

Ellie experienced her share of tragedy. After her family lost their plantation in Georgia at the end of the war and journeyed west, they opened a successful general store in Kansas. But they met trouble when a twister took both her parents and the store. She was a young woman then. Her loveliness drew attractive suitors, but she was lured into a seedy life of easy cash as a saloon girl. Ellie was popular and wise for her age then. She traveled around the Southeast and Midwest. She'd seen enough sadness and searched for land of her own. She scrimped and saved until she saw a saloon for sale in Texas. Ellie stole her fellow saloon girls from another dance hall and brought them to Iris with a steady stream of clientele from the railroad yard.

Then the town changed dramatically. Few of her girls stayed after the shootouts began and Drasco's rude gang wanted more than what they were paying for. With Riley dead, the townspeople were leery of coming in for a drink. Business ground to a halt. A decent number of tables were filled for Saturday night poker and the trains brought some guests, but for how long? Ellie was forty now, way past a time when most saloon girls hung up their satin dresses. After a moment of silence, she queried Kate, "How's business with the rail?"

Kate hid her newfound knowledge of the rail office's impending demise. "Fine, the same. A hole though without Riley." Strax whimpered at the mention of Riley's name.

"Damn shame, what a good man he was." Ellie paused for a moment, wondering what he'd been like as a younger man. Kate had been with him since before Ellie arrived. Her curiosity got the best of her, and Ellie pried, "Did you ever, you know?" Ellie's voice trailed off.

Kate was immediately confused at Ellie's probing. "Did I ever what?"

Ellie laughed, amused at Kate's sudden naiveté. "Did you ever have relations? You know, sex?" And she burst into giggles until Kate's grave look made her stop.

"He was not like that," Kate answered simply. "He was like a father to me." She gazed out the saloon window where Riley perished. She was on the verge of tears.

"Oh Kate, I am sorry," Ellie whispered. "It's just you were always with him. I didn't mean to upset you."

"I know. It's just been difficult." Her eyes wetted with tears and her throat tightened.

Ellie felt bad for hurting Kate's feelings. Her heart was laden for a moment. She hated to see such a kind person suffer such an excruciating loss. She changed the subject as she smoothed her hair and toyed with the collar of her dress. "Well, you know, that young Ferris is quite smitten with you," she eased with her sweet southern lilt.

Kate was bemused. "Yep, he's got quite a yearning, but he's not for me."

"You wouldn't settle down with a young dandy gent like him?" she merrily teased.

"No." Kate twittered. "I don't know what I'm doing." She hadn't decided. As her mind wandered, Kate remembered the invitation and the stash in her pocket. She'd hide it before things got out of hand.

"Honey, your mind is miles away from here." Ellie teased at the adrift look in Kate's eyes.

"I'm sorry, Ellie, I must go. Chores to handle before bed." Kate didn't elaborate; she had to mull it all over. She intended to open that package.

"Well, here's payment for the pump fix. Thanks." With worry wrinkling her forehead, Ellie handed her payment. She hoped that Kate would leave Iris alive in one piece.

"Thanks, El, take care of yourself." Kate moseyed out into the setting sunlight with Strax dutifully behind. She stood for a moment and stared at the gorgeous multicolored sky, full of oranges, pinks, gold, and purples. She muttered to herself, "Someday I will watch the sunset and not give a damn about what tomorrow brings."

7 WOUNDS

Kate undressed at her washstand. It was a simple brown solid pine waist-high table with a porcelain wash bowl. An oval mirror was mounted on top, and a drawer was hidden underneath. She caught herself in the mirror and it still shocked her. Not her age, her hair, or her weight; it was entirely, horribly different.

Kate spent the early evening examining the invitation. She caressed the paper, the card, the twine, and the brown wrapping. Her fingers pressed over the imprinted seal.

Impressive, someone went into a lot of trouble to find me.

She stewed, braiding and fixing her hair over and over. Then pacing across the groaning floor boards. Strax whined and scampered along the bed with her.

Could it be from home? A past she succeeded in leaving behind?

Part of that past was staring back at her in the mirror now. Few had seen them—only two people in Iris—the physical scars that furrowed up, down, and across her spine. Kate threw on the silken night gown that Ming gave to her to cover up the once painful whip lines etched into her back. The cloth made her skin feel luxurious. It was smooth, even against the reddened skin tissue. The gown was an extremely generous gift from Ming and Chin, given after their unexpected revealing dip in the creek at the edge of town.

Kate closed her eyes and remembered how those scars came to be.

St. Louis, Missouri, 1865

"Katherine Louise Church, come in and finish your studies." Henry Church called to his firstborn. Katherine was born on October 5, 1859, to a decent, well-bred couple in St. Louis, Missouri. The daughter of Henry and Alexa Church was a happy, curious child. "You can play later on when you complete your spelling sheet."

Henry had returned home from work. He was a banker in the growing city founded by French and German fur traders. The banks of the muddy Mississippi made the Midwestern town an ideal stop for Westward expansion. Caves underground provided cool storage for a plethora of goods and supplies. It was a city ripe for business, and Henry's employer was prospering.

Henry brushed his fingers through his auburn hair as Katherine galloped towards the door. "Ah, there's my angel."

"Hello, papa!" Kate hugged around her father's knees.

"Go on and finish. Maybe I'll tell you a story when you're done." The gentleman spoke with a gleam in his stunning green eyes. He came from sturdy Irish ancestry.

"Don't spoil her too much," Alexa called from the sitting room. The daughter of well-to-do Polish immigrants was alabaster-skinned, blonde-haired, and blue-eyed with a petite, curvy frame. Katherine was her spitting image and the sole recipient of her parents' kind love and attention.

That is, until surprisingly, ten years later, her younger sister Abigail was born. However, Katherine wasn't jealous. Instead, her sibling became her favorite doll and she reveled in caring for Abigail. She dressed her sister for tea parties and nicknamed her Abby. But the family's perfect life was soon shattered.

"Katherine, take Abby upstairs. Martha, if you could make sure the girls get settled for the night, I'd appreciate it." Henry spoke haltingly after stepping out of his bedroom.

Unfortunately for the Church family, their bliss ended during Alexa's struggle to give birth to a third child. Both she and the baby perished. Katherine was twelve and Abigail was only two. Even at their tender ages, they saw that their father was broken.

"Papa? Mama?" Abby babbled as Martha and Katherine tucked the toddler in.

"Go to sleep child." Martha cooed.

"We'll play tomorrow." Katherine choked back tears.

Worse still, the country was in slow recovery from a war with itself. Henry's bank closed when the owners fearfully stole all their assets and ran North. Henry collected himself to care for his family and found employment with a rail line loading box cars. His demotion from white-collar worker to hard laborer was a blow to the proud head of the Church clan.

They retained a literate servant, Martha, who cared for the girls. She was gifted to them by a kind, wealthy neighbor, Mr. Parker.

"I know you're in a struggle Henry. Martha loves those girls. I'd like for her to stay with you, as long as you need her." Mr. Parker sat with Henry in the family's parlor. He was empathetic for his neighbor who'd gone from astute businessman to blue-collar stock.

"I appreciate it. Things haven't been the same with Alexa gone." Henry poured a second brandy as the gentlemen talked business.

Martha was a pleasant black woman, with generous dimples. Her long braids were kept up in a neat bonnet and she dressed in crisp aprons and simple gray house dresses.

As the years passed, Katherine attended a church school and was a brilliant student. She found solace in religious learning. She and Martha tended to the home and Abby, as Henry toiled for long days.

But cruel fate intervened when two years later, a stack of crates fell off a boxcar, nearly crushing Henry.

"Your pa will never be the same. You'll have to help more Katherine." Martha whispered as she put a cool cloth on Henry's forehead. He was out cold from heavy syrup that the doctor supplied in blue apothecary bottles.

He was permanently crippled from the waist down and never worked another day in his life. The Church family was in dire straits.

"Katherine, can you tidy up these papers? Then take these lemonades out to the coachmen?"

"Yes, Sir." In desperation, Katherine found employment from Mr. Parker, the same man who gave Martha to the Church family. Mr. Parker owned a group of livery stables and carriage businesses that kept stalls and horses for prominent citizens. Kate cleaned and cooked for Mr. Parker, a widower, and his son

Michael, who was seven years older than Katherine. It was Michael that began calling Katherine by her nickname, Kate.

The Parkers were attractive, wealthy men. Michael reflected the striking appearance of his father with deep brown eyes, wavy black hair, and a well-kept mustache. Both were over six feet in height. Mr. Parker groomed Michael to run the successful family business. He was learning from the bottom up, frequently cleaning the stables and the tack room and attending to the carriages. Despite the daily grind, he was good-natured and always had a smile for Kate.

Kate was fairly compensated by the Parkers, and she enjoyed working for them except for an unavoidable troubled individual.

The head driver and manager over the stables, a Mr. McKendrick, was a burly, drunken Irishman with unruly reddish hair and a ruddy beard. He possessed a cautious temper that flared unceremoniously, but his efficiency with tools and the carriages made him invaluable to the Parkers. He'd rudely ogle Kate. After school, Kate cooked dinner for the Parkers and sent a plate to McKendrick and his equally rakish brother, Peter, another driver for the Parkers. She hated this task. His eyes flashed and leered over her body as she brought them dinner in the office. He snickered with his sibling in between rides. This was noted by one of the Parkers' better servants, Silas.

Silas was Martha's brother. He wore the same happy expression and demeanor as his sister. He was a broad, solid man, and was a well-dressed servant to the Parkers. Just before the war, Mr. Parker purchased Silas and Martha after a wealthy plantation owner visiting St. Louis died unexpectedly. His widow did not have room or means to ship them back South, which forced her to have a male relative put them up for sale before returning home.

Silas and Martha were literate and well-groomed. Although the kind-hearted Mr. Parker did not need both of them, he didn't want to separate the siblings. After the War Between the States was over, he offered Martha to the Churches. Mr. Parker even covered her salary when Mr. Church took ill. They were permitted to visit.

On these occasions, Silas told Martha of McKendrick's behavior around young Kate, but they otherwise kept silent. "He's a nasty man," Silas warned.

"Yes, he is, but can't say much. Just keep an eye on him." Martha agreed.

McKendrick was known to whip unruly slaves before the war. Mr. Parker demanded he stop this punishment after emancipation, but they still feared him. However, Martha and Silas watched over Kate as much as possible without starting any trouble. Kate also had a protector and friend in Michael Parker.

Michael often loaned Kate books from Mr. Parker's library and taught her how to care for horses. As her skills grew, he taught her how to train and ride. It was in these moments that Kate forgot her troubles. She liked taking the reins and feeling the wind in her hair during a spirited ride on the Parkers' grounds. Kate learned the power of a well-made whip and felt empowered with its use. She longed for a better life and forgot that McKendrick's impolite stares made her uncomfortable.

As Kate grew into her middle teens, her heart warmed at the sight of Michael. He smiled warmly and tipped his hat in passing. He was in the stables less and the Parkers' office often, learning the business side of the family's employment. Unfortunately, this meant that Kate ran into McKendrick if she went to see the horses. It made her stomachache to be in his presence. She sought refuge in rides to a pond on the Parkers' property. It was a gorgeous lake, with a dock. It was delightfully hidden by maples and oak trees that offered their sturdy branches over the fresh waters. After a meal and clean-up at the Parkers', Kate took one of the horses out to relax by the cool water, disrobing and swimming before assisting Martha with Abby and her father at home.

Behind the trees surrounding the pristine water, McKendrick naughtily spied on Kate. This salaciousness began on a quiet evening after dinner, when he saw Kate leave on a horse from the livery. He stalked her and found her secret place of serenity. Since then, he wickedly pleasured himself in the greenery as she relaxed and dreamed in the water. In the pond, Kate never saw her interloper. She was becoming troubled of late, preoccupied with her family, and desperately desired to be alone.

"Awe Miss Kate, a tax collector came by today. He left a bill." Martha fixed supper in the hot kitchen.

"Alright then, I'll get to the bank tomorrow and see what I can do." Kate cleaned up and tried not to worry.

The Churches were further in debt. Kate brought home pay, but it wasn't enough to support them. Henry was treated with all kinds of potions, doctors, and elixirs, but lacked improvement to his paralysis. Martha was gifted to them, but with the Civil War long settled and no funds coming in, the Churches might lose her services.

Earlier that day Mr. Parker pulled Kate aside. "I spoke to your pa about offering Martha and Silas complete freedom when the country's upheaval is truly over. I'm not completely sure he understood me, Kate. Silas and Martha are open to the opportunity to leave to find better pay at jobs further north of St. Louis." His words bounced in Kate's brain as she poked at her food.

New presidents endeavored to heal the country's wounds after Lincoln was assassinated and the country was pulling itself from turmoil.

Kate perused the paper once she finished eating. The next day, after she'd taken out as much money as she could from the bank, she ran over to the job postings outside the market for additional employment. "Jobs today! Go West!" A large sign caught her eye. She had just enough time to walk over to the railroad office.

"Howdy, there miss." A rail director greeted her.

After a few moments of honest words about her talents and a fib about her age, Kate received an offer for a job as a rail secretary in Texas. "Just come on back when you're ready. The position is open for thirty days." The director winked as she trotted out.

But why am I scared of being so far away? She bemoaned as she returned to work for the Parkers. Kate tired of waiting for the town to get better and dreamed of finding a new life. Henry became despondent and drank heavily. Unbeknownst to Kate, he prepared to find a suitor with interest in her and possibly marry her off. But he didn't have a dowry to offer a prospective groom.

"We have to curtail Henry's drinking. I don't know how he keeps getting the liquor. And he's not making sound decisions. Poor Kate is working herself to death." Martha spoke to Silas about how she might cure Henry. "I'll start watering down his medications. That poor soul might give up Kate to anyone."

Unfortunately, McKendrick overheard this exchange. He'd started to follow Kate home and hid in the shrubbery around the house, spying on the Church family.

Only a week later, he'd use it to his advantage over Henry. That day of hideous subversion had been unusually hot for June. The moment Kate left for a swim after working all day in the stables and Martha went to gather vegetables from the garden, McKendrick stole into the Church home and caught Henry unawares.

For most of that day, Kate had toiled away to keep the drivers and horses cooled upon their return from broiling rides in the beating sunshine. She lugged water and food to the staff continuously.

After a quick bribe of Henry, McKendrick was off, busy transferring a particularly important shipment from a steamboat to a train as Mr. Parker was supervising the robust crew.

Michael was frequently in and out of the stables that day. He kept asking Kate about how she was holding up. When the drivers left for a third run of shipment, he took her aside. "Kate, you're flushed. You're thirsty, aren't you? Need a drink?" He queried kindly.

Kate shyly beamed in return. "Yes, I do. Thank you."

Michael poured her a cup from a bucket she'd just brought in. "Here you go." He handed her the water, and she drank gratefully. Then, unexpectedly, he dipped a clean cloth in the bucket and wiped her brow.

Kate was embarrassed but relaxed at his attentiveness and closed her eyes.

"Your cheeks are far too pink. Sit for a moment." He took her hand and led her to the office. "Wait here," he kindly offered her a chair. "I'll be right back."

Kate breathed for a moment to steady her nerves and drank from the cup. *He is unbearably kind.*

Michael returned with a loaf of bread and fruit from the Parker mansion. "Here, I gather you hadn't eaten either."

"Yes, thank you." Kate blushed. Her heart was beating harder than usual, and she felt warmth rising through her skin.

Michael watched her eat. She had become lovely. Kate was still young, but he noticed that she was no longer the neighbor girl that cooked for his family.

"Kate how is your father?" he inquired.

"The same. Morose for the most part, otherwise he'll play games and tutor Abby with Martha. I know he feels bad that he can't assist." She felt horrible about her father's situation.

"Well Kate, you are doing well for him and your family. What are your aspirations after finishing school?" Michael observed. Secretly, he wanted Kate to reveal if she had any dreams, or if Henry even betrothed her. The Churches were in serious financial trouble. He worried for her safety and desired her for himself.

"I don't know," she stuttered, wide-eyed. "I haven't had time to plan." She set down her plate and cup, then wrung her hands in consternation.

Michael reached over and covered Kate's fretful fingers. "Kate, if you ever require anything, please ask me. I know my father would be glad to help." And before Michael expressed how he cared for her; the carriages returned for fresh horses. "Well then." He took her hand to assist her in standing. "Back to work!"

The remainder of the day sped by. Soon, all the horses were resting, and the drivers went home. McKendrick, Michael, and Mr. Parker went over several shipping papers in the office. It had been a profitable day.

Martha delivered sandwiches for the Parkers, and they ate in the office as McKendrick and his brother left.

"Come eat," Michael urged Kate, and they enjoyed refreshments.

"Well done!" Mr. Parker exclaimed as the meal was finished and waved at Kate as he departed for home.

"You can go, Kate," Michael spoke tiredly. "I have paperwork to finish. I'll see you tomorrow." He handed Kate her pay and then waved her towards the door with a grin.

"Thank you!" she exclaimed happily, pocketing her earnings. Kate rushed away to wash. The sun was near setting, but she still desired a swim. She left the horses behind, ran to the pond, and undressed on the bank. The lush green trees swayed with a gentle late-day breeze as she eased into the calm lake. The blue-green waters enveloped her skin as mallards swam lazily on the other side. She floated on her back, gazing up at the rich blue sky, her young breasts bobbing as her lithe arms and legs extended. For a moment, she was blissful and forgot about the world outside of the forest.

But memories of Michael wandered in. He had been kind, such a gentleman.

What would she do after school? She'd find work, marry, or do both?

Kate's mind was tired, and she had to go home; she'd lost track of time. Kate came out of her peaceful float on the water.

When she stood, she saw Michael watching at the edge of the pond, his mouth open. She froze, gasped, and backed into the water, embarrassed. "Michael, I'm sorry—I shouldn't be swimming in the pond, I know..." she stuttered.

"Wait, Kate. It's okay. I was coming in for a swim myself." He laughed and his brown eyes twinkled naughtily. He stripped down hastily on the bank and approached the dock. His skin was golden in the setting sun.

Kate stared despite striving to turn away. She flushed in recognition of his beauty. She'd seen nudes in art books from the Parker library but had never seen a man in the flesh. In historic periods, Michael Parker may have well been a DaVinci's muse. He was tall, lean, and very much a man. He jumped in from the dock and was under the water.

Kate hesitated. *Where is he?*

She shrieked with a pinch on her bottom, and he surfaced next to her.

"Isn't the water lovely?" he whispered.

She managed to nod. Kate felt an ache, a desire she would not feel again for a long, long time after this day. But this moment, she never forgot, for she realized she was in love with Michael Parker. Her body quivered pleasantly as tender warmth ran along her skin.

"Don't be afraid, Kate." Michael put his arms around her.

She held her breath. The world had stopped.

"I promise you; I will care for you. You and your family." He pulled her chin into his hands and placed a slow tender kiss on her lips. Cool drops from his black tendrils fell onto her cheeks.

Her body wobbled and he put his hands on her back, steadying her. His body was firm whilst flush with hers.

"Tomorrow Kate, I will talk to my father, then ask your papa for your hand. You have grown into a lovely woman, and I cannot bear to be away from my sweetheart."

She choked, this revelation from Michael flummoxed her.

"You won't have to work so hard Kate, just say yes."

She'd swear she was dreaming, but he was here with her, skin on skin. Cool ripples of the water lapped their bodies, reflecting the sky which turned shades of teal, blue, and purple.

"Yes—I will." Kate wept. She had been lonely, always sweating away, and not having true friends. *Father will always be ill*. Abby was a child and Michael had pledged his aid. Refusal of such a grand proposal was not an option. She felt her body collapsing and released into his hold.

"Don't be upset. Here, wrap your legs around me." He caressed her. He hardened against her as he lifted her up and out of the pond.

Despite his warm demeanor, Michael was still a young, impatient man and seduced Kate that late afternoon. He placed Kate on her back in the cool grass on the edge of the pond, lay next to her, and cooed. "Kate, you will be my wife, and I will honor you, but you must obey me, you must trust me. And at this moment I must know that you will give yourself to me, no others, you understand?"

"Yes." She had wondered about men and sex. Now he was prepared to teach her. The ache of desire spread over her body as if it were tinged with fire. The pale white of her skin flushed a rosy pink.

"Relax, be still," Michael murmured as he kissed her. His hands teased her body. "It might sting at first, but you will like it," he cooed in her ear.

Her heart pounded in her head like the thunder of horses running wild. She felt his hand slip below her waist to delicately touch her. *Yes*, Kate moaned and exhaled sharply with pain. Passion overcame her as he made love to her in the grass.

Afterward, he held her tight as the stars peeked through the darkening sky. Michael spoke of how wonderful their life would be and he promised he'd be a kind husband.

Kate felt as though she'd been in a peaceful slumber.

Not so kind were McKendrick and his brother, hidden in trees along the pond. They watched the two during their intimacy. McKendrick's blood boiled in a jealous rage. When Michael and Kate dressed, the two men disappeared into the darkness.

Kate accepted Michael's proposal, but only hours before, McKendrick asked Henry Church for his eldest daughter's hand after drugging him with whisky laced with absinthe. Henry, out of his mind and drunk, agreed, especially when he couldn't offer a dowry. In a stupor, he signed a document he knew nothing of, but it spelled out that Mr. Church had not only given Kate to McKendrick but all property of the Churchs as well.

Michael and Kate returned to the barns in the moonlight. The last pleasant memory of that day was holding Michael's hand as he prepared to open the door to the largest barn on the property.

Without warning, her world went pitch black. Shortly thereafter, Kate awoke, the dust of the barn stinging her eyes, accompanied by a fierce headache. She blinked and her vision adjusted to the low haze of an oil lamp off to her right. Her wrists hurt.

Why are my hands above my head? Her foggy mind wondered. She coughed and gradually realized that she was tied to a post in the barn, half kneeling in the hay and dirt.

"Y'er awake now, eh?" A low voice slurred from near the lamp. Kate turned her head over her shoulder to see McKendrick sitting on a stool, smoking a pipe and drinking whisky. "Thought you'd just get your bloomers in a mess with the owner's son, didn't you now? Well, that ain't happening," he threatened hoarsely. He picked up a riding crop from a nearby post and pointed it at Michael's dead body, still oozing blood from a deep gash in his head. The horses whinnied and Kate was overwhelmed with sickness. "Look what you made me do, ya lil' cunt. Be punished, kept in line, see? I'm gonna make sure this don't happen again." He tossed the crop aside and staggered from the stool to a stall next to Kate. McKendrick reached for a bull whip hanging from a brass hook.

He stalked over, grabbed the back of her neck, and goaded in her ear, "Bitch. You're gonna learn. This is for your own good." And with that he grabbed the backside collar of her dress and ripped it open, exposing Kate's upper back. Violently he yanked down her corset from behind her and ran his dirty hands over her naked breasts. The smell of whisky on his breath and an apparent bump on the head overtook her. Her head fell to the post, and she began to sob. Kate weakened with no fight left in her.

"Shut up whore!" McKendrick bellowed and backed away. She fell into unconsciousness again, but it was the intense pain of a bullwhip snapped from his hand, cutting into her flesh that forced her awake. It cracked loudly, forcing her vision to become clouded with stars. Her unworldly scream echoed through the barn.

Strax and the Widow

Kate leaned to the post as blood trickled down her spine. "No, no, no! Please, God, no!" she begged.

But he leaned back, having picked up Michael Parker's bullwhip, and struck her repeatedly. She screamed out hysterically with each brutal lash. She scrambled to stand but her legs collapsed under her. Kate's throat was dry, and as he whipped her another three times, her screams became rusty and choked. The seven gashes in her back stung like a thousand bees. Her ears roared and the world was near black. *I am going to die, whipped like a defenseless animal by a vicious demon.* It seemed like hell erupted all around.

As McKendrick leaned back for an eighth strike, he lost his balance and drunkenly fell to the table. The oil lamp crashed to the floor and set the barn ablaze. The flaming liquid splattered his dusty suit. He was on fire, running and screaming until collapsing in a nook filled with hay dry from the heat. It combusted immediately, shooting flames to the roof and the other stalls. Smoke and ash filled the barn. The horses were bucking wildly, thumping hard along the walls. Kate was sliding under as flames licked around the post to which she had been tied.

Fortunately, Martha had overheard McKendrick as he'd cheated a drunken Mr. Church. She'd heard voices after she'd come inside from picking vegetables for soup. She quivered behind the kitchen door as McKendrick forced Kate's poor papa to sign bogus papers.

"Lord have mercy. That poor girl!" She whispered and ran to the Parkers' to warn Silas with a plan to protect Kate.

Mr. Parker retired early with no idea that his business was burning to the ground. As Martha approached the Parkers' estate, she saw a golden glow on the trees around the property and an acrid burning smell.

Silas had been washing up when he heard screams. He glanced out from the servants' quarters to see fire dancing its way through the main stable. He dashed from the Parkers' home to release the horses. As he raced through the burning barn, opening stalls and pushing out horses, he was stunned to see Kate tied up and wounded. And at the other end, through the thickening smoke, he saw Michael Parker strewn on the floor. He untied Kate just as her body was giving up, slumping in severe pain. Silas picked her up, haphazardly bent over to get under the smoke and flames. Kate's right hand skimmed the floor as he began to stumble through the smoke and fire. As they passed the discarded whip, Kate forced her eyes open. She instinctively grabbed it and dragged the bullwhip through the dirt as Silas ran with her. That whip belonged to Michael.

He needs it, her impaired mind reasoned.

Silas carried Kate outside to Martha, who wiped her with her apron and then covered her with a riding blanket. "C'mon child!" she urged, and Kate coughed awake.

"Martha, we must go home. It's bad, really bad. I'll tell you what happened." Kate gasped upon recognizing the fear in Martha's eyes. The Church's housekeeper had never heard Kate utter how bad their situation was, even when she toiled hard, and they slowly sold off items from their home to keep up appearances.

Silas returned to the fiery enclosure for Michael when it collapsed. The roof timbers groaned and fell in a mighty terrible roar. Flames shot high in the air and smoke poured out from the destroyed structure. Neighbors and firemen were arriving in a flurry, including McKendrick's brother Peter passed out drunk in the woods nearby. His sibling waited for Kate and Michael to return. He fell out from a tangle of shrubbery and with a muddled mind wondered where his foolish older brother was.

Martha and Kate managed to hurry to the Church's home before anyone else saw them. Peter searched for a moment, but as others arrived, he believed that the elder McKendrick perished, as he had been in the barn.

But who set the fire? It was probably the bitch's fault he fumed. But then he saw Silas putting out the flames that ignited dry brush near the barn.

Hmm, that fool and his sister were always whispering. Maybe they planned to burn everything down and escape with the Parkers' property?

Silas finished stomping out cinders that flew astray, as the mass of fire that was once the barns, continued to burn. A bucket brigade of neighbors attempted to control it and the firemen readied their hoses. He peeked up to see Peter watching him. The McKendrick's never liked him, and a shiver went down Silas's spine. Peter glared at him savagely. Sensing the younger McKendrick's fury, Silas panicked and ran for the Church's residence.

Peter yelled loudly over the crackling flames, "Hey, over there, he set the blaze!" Heads turned from the line of fire volunteers. Mr. Parker arrived at the ruined stables to see his most trusted servant running away to shouts of Peter's accusations.

Peter McKendrick approached Mr. Parker. "You know those former slaves were up to something." He growled just enough to put suspicion in Mr. Parker's mind.

Silas was frightened, his head pounding as he tore across the Parker property and past several other estates to the Church's residence. His mind raced.

Would Mr. Parker believe that he came to put out the fire? How had Kate and Michael been put in peril? Michael died in the inferno. Where was McKendrick?

He couldn't make sense of any of it except he'd just been accused of burning the barns down. They'd lynch him and maybe Martha too. He burst through the gate of the Church's mansion and rapped on the rear door to the kitchen. "Martha, Martha!" he yelled. "Let me in. We gotta run!" It seemed like forever before she opened the door to reveal a bloodied and filthy Kate, crouching on a stool near the washstand. She held a soggy cloth, having finished cleaning Kate's shredded back.

"What in God's name is happening?" Martha exclaimed. Silas's eyes were white with fear and sweat poured through his clothes. He was panting heavily. Remnants of the fire and ash covered his body. He coughed hoarsely and moaned, dropping to his knees in exhaustion.

"That younger McKendrick, Peter, he said I burnt down the barns, killed his brother." Silas grasped onto the wooden preparation table in the center of the kitchen to support himself. Martha soaked a rag in the washstand and handed it to her panicked brother.

"That's not true!" Martha exclaimed. "That filthy driver tried to kill Miss Kate! The drunken fool ambushed her and Michael. He nearly whipped her to death."

Kate motioned to Silas. She told Martha what transpired when they arrived back at the Church's home.

Strax and the Widow

"Martha, let's leave, they'll be here any minute," Silas urged and peeked out the kitchen window. "They'll be coming for me."

"Miss Kate can explain. Maybe they'll listen?" Martha quivered. "She can show them the wounds. Tell them the truth?"

Kate sputtered, "Where's Michael?" Her head was heavy with searing pain. She couldn't see straight. It was as if there were two Martha's and Silas' in the kitchen.

"Sister, they aren't listening," he bemoaned to Martha. He turned to Kate, and spoke softly, "The young Mr. Parker, Michael, he was still in the barn when it collapsed. I'm sorry I didn't save him, Miss Kate."

Kate whimpered in pain. Noises of discord were heard in the distance.

"Alright, we can figure this out later," Martha hatched a plan. "Turn out that lamp!" Silas obeyed and they were blanketed only in the moonlight. "Let's get upstairs, in the dark, where we can't be seen. Miss Kate, we'll put you in bed, say you been asleep all evening after being at the stables today. No one alive knows you were in that barn tonight." Martha wiped her down in the dark and threw a house coat over her as she spoke. "You'll have to lay on your back and pretend those wounds don't exist in case they come peeking in. Now, go on upstairs. I'll check on you after I handle this." Kate summoned her remaining strength to stumble through the mansion and crawled upstairs.

"Silas, strip down, give me your clothes." Martha's eyes adjusted to the dark. She took a cloth from the linen closet and handed it to Silas. She wiped off any soot, then took his clothes, Kate's shredded dress, the dirty rags, and stuffed them into the wood stove. They wouldn't be searching in a cold oven. The voices outside were getting louder. With a discreet peek, Martha saw the dots of lanterns coming down the street. They were searching the yards of other homes. "Let's hurry, upstairs!" she whispered. She grabbed Silas's hand and guided him toward the stairs. As they passed the parlor, she saw Mr. Church, highlighted by the fireplace, still drugged, slouched sideways in an armchair and papers on the table. "Up, I'll meet you on the second floor!" she urged her brother.

Martha tip-toed into the parlor and found that McKendrick, in his haste to corner Kate with news of their impending nuptials, foolishly left the corrupt marriage contract right next to Mr. Church. He was probably drunk himself, Martha mused. He'd even left the alcohol bottle behind. She picked up the papers and tossed them into the fire as Mr. Church snored heavily. No one would know McKendrick's dirty trick he'd played on the Church family. He was dead and the papers were consumed by the flames. She picked up an empty bottle of the absinthe that the rotten McKendrick used to drug Henry. She strode upstairs where Silas waited, still wrapped in the tablecloth.

"I can hear them." He spoke lowly and in a panic. "What took you so long?"

"In here," Martha gestured, "the child's room." They crept into Abigail's bedroom. At the foot of the young Church's bed was a beat-up steamer trunk that Martha used to store blankets and toys. Efficiently she emptied it and motioned him in. "Just stay quiet, I'm making certain the little one won't wake." As if on cue, Abigail stirred. Martha dipped her finger on the rim of the absinthe bottle, sat on the bed, and brushed the girl's lips with a dab of the sweet, drowsy drink. Instinctively, the child licked and with a satisfied smile, fell into a deeper sleep.

Silas just barely fit into the trunk but folded himself enough to tuck completely in. Martha closed the lid, locked it, and tucked the key into her pocket.

She closed the door, and crossed the hall, in darkness to Kate's room. Kate managed to put on a dressing gown and slid into the bed. "Miss Kate, are you okay now?"

"It's painful, but I'll manage," she moaned. Martha tucked her in and placed a night cap on her head.

"Here, drink this." Martha offered her the absinthe. Kate sipped the drops. "Try to sleep. I'll hold them off at the door, but if they come up, you've been here since after dinner." Kate acknowledged Martha's demands. Despite the sting of her wounds, she drifted to slumber just as the neighbors rapped on the door. No one stirred and Martha waited. An insistent knock followed. Martha rose from Kate's bed, left the room, shut the door, then checked her dress and apron. She put on a robe, tucked the apron in its pocket, and slipped down the stairs. The banging was louder as she cautiously approached the door. *I can do this*, Martha encouraged herself. *I have to do this for Silas, for Mr. Church, Kate, and Abigail*, she resolved and opened the door.

Mr. Parker and several of the neighborhood men stood on the porch with lanterns illuminating their faces in an orange glow. Mr. Parker spoke sternly, "Martha, are the Churches home? Have you seen Silas, your brother?"

"No sir," she replied with such serenity that she convinced herself. "I just gave Mr. Church his medicine and the ladies have been in bed since after dinner." She was still holding the absinthe as if she'd just doled out a portion. The men peered inside. Martha opened the door wide so they could see for themselves. Peeking from behind might rouse their suspicion.

"May we come in? We have an urgent matter to discuss with Mr. Church." Mr. Parker didn't believe that Silas was hiding, that he may have burnt down the barn as a distraction to escape. But he had to see.

"Do come in please." She motioned politely.

Mr. Parker spoke to the men, "Take a gander around and come back to the porch. We'll go inside." He and two others crept into the Church residence as Martha turned on gaslights and led them to the parlor. Mr. Church was still passed out. Martha shook him to no avail and then turned to the visitors.

"I apologize Mr. Parker; he was in fierce pain today and the doctor prescribed heavy syrup. He's been sleeping since dinner." Martha kindly covered him with a quilt from the sofa.

"I see," Mr. Parker mumbled. It was obvious that Henry hadn't heard. He pitied his neighbor who had once been a vibrant happy man but was now reduced to a sad sack of a human being. He glared directly at Martha, "Have you seen Silas tonight?"

"Oh no sir, not since dinner. He'd left to finish up at the stables."

She seemed sincere, but Mr. Parker was both furious and grieving. His son and best driver were dead, and the largest stable burnt to the ground. He pressed Martha for details. "And where's Katherine?"

"She went upstairs directly after coming home, sir. She was exhausted." Martha was steady in her reserve. She wisely distracted the men with a query, "Sir, may I ask what's wrong?"

"A terrible fire at the estate. The main barn burnt down. Michael and Mr. McKendrick were killed, and Silas is missing." Mr. Parker blanched as the other folk peeked outside the parlor.

Strax and the Widow

"Oh sir, that's horrible!" Martha exclaimed. She channeled her fear for Silas into genuine tears for Michael. "Oh my, Miss Kate, she will be so distraught."

"May we check upstairs?" he inquired. He motioned for the other two men to stay behind. They gingerly poked around the spotless first floor and found nothing.

"Oh, yes sir, this way." Martha wept but succinctly led Mr. Parker upstairs. Silas heard the footsteps but didn't flinch. The trunk had scant holes and was hot and stuffy. Martha opened the door to Kate's room and was relieved to see that Kate was in a deep sleep, her hand tucked under her pillow. She leaned in to wake Kate, but Mr. Parker stopped her, touching Martha's shoulder.

"Let her rest. Tomorrow will be a hard day," Mr. Parker moaned in a choked whisper.

"Sir, I am sorry, I know Miss Kate was fond of Michael." Martha's voice trailed. "Can I offer you a drink?"

"No, no, back downstairs." He turned and walked out to the hall. He paused. "Whose room is this?"

"Why that's Miss Abigail's room. Would you like to see it?" And smartly, Martha opened the door. No one hiding a slave would be so bold. "Isn't she a cherub?" Abigail was a pleasant girl, her auburn curls framing her pink chubby cheeks.

Mr. Parker only made a cursory glance into the room. Seeing Henry's child only further reminded him that his only son was dead.

"Yes, well, um, thank you." He went back downstairs without waiting for Martha and opened the front door. He directed the others. "Let's keep searching outside." Several horses were spared, roaming wild after the fire. They whinnied and tumbled in the street, sensing the discord of their master. Mr. Parker turned back to the doorway. "Thank you, Martha. I'll be back round tomorrow to talk to Mr. Church. Be safe and lock up. You must tell me if Silas comes around, you understand?"

"Yes sir, I will," Martha lied convincingly.

"Goodnight then." He tipped his hat. Mr. Parker left brokenhearted as the freed horses were rounded up and the neighbors and volunteers returned to their homes, the fire having been put out. Martha closed the door and slid down the inside, quietly fussing. Mr. Parker had been kind to them, but Silas was right. He'd been accused, with no other choice but to run. Martha and Silas didn't sleep that night.

"Come on now." She let him out of the trunk and passed clean clothes to Silas.

"I've never been so scared in my life. How am I going to get out of here?" Silas finished dressing. They sat in the dark of the kitchen, whispering of an escape for him.

"The Underground Railroad still has hiding places in nearby Alton, Illinois if we can get you there." Martha laid out some food and copious amounts of water.

"What's that?" Silas gasped. They were startled by movement outside.

Martha jumped up and peered through the kitchen curtains to see one of the Parker's steeds rustling in the yard.

"It's a horse," Martha exclaimed. It was as if God heard her silent prayers. She ran out, tied the lost beast to the gate, and distracted him with apples.

Silas kept watch from the house, fresh beads of sweat glistening on his forehead.

Martha rushed back in. "We at least have a piece of the plan now. We've got a ride; you won't be able to go out on your own. If anyone recognizes you on Mr. Parker's horse, you'd be dead. Kate or Mr. Church might get you to the docks?" Martha urged.

"Mr. Church is in no condition to leave the house." Silas shook his head.

"Kate hasn't fully come to terms with last night's peril. But after she had rested?" Martha surmised.

Their talk turned to dreams of escape for Silas until the eastern sky brightened and Martha heard a stirring upstairs. She ordered Silas, "Hide in the linen closet in the kitchen, I'll investigate."

Fortunately, it was Kate awakening due to the aching of the slashes on her back. They dried into grotesque scabs that stuck to her nightdress. She sat up, still woozy, and her eyes adjusted to the bedroom. For a moment Kate wondered if she dreamt it—the hard work, the swim, the lovemaking, the fire, and the horrible loss. But stranger still, she was holding onto something.

Kate gazed down to see that she was still clutching Michael's bullwhip under her pillow. She released it for a moment, the dried blood and ash embedded in its leather braid imprinting her palm, and began to weep. It was all she had left of Michael. Martha approached, sat on the bed, and held the distraught teen.

"Oh Miss Kate, it'll be alright," Martha soothed. "You did right. Mr. Parker came by after you fell asleep and didn't see any trouble. I hid Silas in Abigail's steam trunk. But he'll be back later today. You must be strong, and we must get Silas to safety. Can we get him to Alton? We have a horse that escaped from the fire. He's tied up in the yard." Kate understood.

"What time is it?" Kate inquired. "Is anybody else awake?"

"Five a.m., miss. Everyone is still sleeping," Martha replied wearily. The long night and day before had caught up with her.

Kate snapped awake. "We must hurry. I can get Silas down to the river docks. I'll have him shipped upriver. I know a man that used to work with father, Robert Campbell, which will arrange his pick-up. We'll put him in that trunk. There's a two-seater buggy in the yard buried under some overgrowth of ivy. Father was selling it, but Mr. Parker asked us to keep it. Help me up." Kate stretched with pain from all the events.

Martha touched her locked hand, still clutching the whip, "Oh Miss Kate, you have to let that go."

A sudden fierceness appeared in Kate's eyes. "No, it's mine." Kate held the whip tighter and grimaced. "Get cloths from the washstand." She ordered Martha to dab the back of her nightdress down with water and then peeled it away from her damaged body. Kate stiffened and bit her lip as she wiped the whip clean. They hastily made a poultice from lard, covered the wounds, and Martha then assisted Kate in dressing.

"Does it hurt, Miss Kate?" Martha asked kindly.

"Like hell." Kate laughed with frustration and Martha twittered. She never cussed before, but Kate experienced a lot of firsts that day. They packed a bag and case for Kate, pulled the steamer trunk from Abby's room, then hurried downstairs racing against the disappearing darkness. Martha let Silas out of the closet, and he collapsed onto the floor.

"Oh Miss Kate!" he exclaimed.

"Shhh," Kate soothed. "My dress, Martha, where is it?"

"It's here, in the stove." Kate marveled at Martha's cleverness as she handed her the shredded material. Miraculously Kate's pay was still rolled up in a pocket. Martha's eyes grew wide at the realization of nearly burning the savings. "Oh my, I almost…"

"I know. Still, burn the dress after I leave. And—" Kate stuffed the dress back into the stove. She then reached up to a round tin container hidden behind dishes on the highest shelf in the china cabinet. After opening the lid, a wad of cash sprang out. "Take this."

"Miss Kate, you've been hiding this?" Martha exclaimed.

"I was saving it for a day like today. We're buying your brother's freedom." Kate handed Silas half the cash. "Let's get you in that trunk."

They crept out to hitch up the horse to the two-seater. The horse was Blaze, her favorite.

He'd followed me home. Kate was bolstered by the horse's memory.

"What a glorious blessing." Martha winked. The trunk fit neatly onto the backside of the buggy. Martha gave Kate information on an address for the Underground in Alton. She knew that Kate possessed the courage to pass through town and deliver her brother to safety. Martha tucked her brother in with a canteen, jerky, and apples. She wept despite desperately trying to contain her emotions.

"No tears sister. We'll meet again, I know," Silas whispered.

"Amen, God bless you!" she cried. Silas kissed her hand, then Martha closed the lid and locked the trunk. Kate hurried inside, took a long look around, and sighed.

She headed upstairs to Abby's room with trepidation. As Kate touched her sister's shoulder, she whispered, "Martha's taking care of you and daddy. I'll come back as soon as I can." Abby stirred for a moment as Kate kissed her cheek, then left, and closed the bedroom door behind her.

After heading downstairs, she dashed off a note for her Father, regarding a terrible accident, that she'd found other employment and she'd be sending funds home, and she'd write when possible. Kate approached the dim parlor. The fire had burnt out and her father slumbered peacefully. Tears rolled down as she tucked the note into his vest and patted his chest. She dabbed her eyes dry and left the only home she'd ever known. The sun was rising over fog as Kate took the reins of the buggy.

"Miss Kate, when you get back from the safe house, what will you do? How will you explain—" Martha was silenced.

"Martha, listen. I'm not coming back for a while. McKendrick's brother is a liar and God knows what he'll say. They can't question me if I'm not here. I left a note for my father, I know I can get work in Texas."

"Texas! Miss Kate!" Martha shook her head.

"You care for father and Abby." Kate handed her the remaining cash. "There's extra in another tin in the cabinet." She hugged Martha tightly. "When they come round today, tell them I was upset and couldn't stay. Do your best, please. I'll send funds when I can. Mr. Parker will step in. He'll see you're upset at the loss of Silas."

Martha attempted to protest, "Miss Kate, oh you can't."

Kate summoned her resolve and appeared older than her sixteen years. "Martha, if they find Silas and react harshly, he'll die. He saved my life, it's my turn to save his. Be careful and hang on. I'll come back when people are better." She was so stern that Martha retreated. "Goodbye, Martha." Kate painfully climbed into the buggy.

"Goodbye, Miss Kate." Martha wept and Kate drove away into the dissipating fog, bullwhip in hand. Within the hour, a steamer trunk had been loaded onto a boat bound for Alton, Illinois. Its carriers had been bribed with a decent amount of dollar bills, a well-bred horse, and a two-seater buggy.

About an hour later, the St. Louis rail office opened to a young woman who had been interviewed before. She was the rail's newest employee and headed on the first train out West. About the same time, Martha was cooking breakfast for the Churches over a stove lined with bad memories that turned to ash.

A couple of hours later, Mr. Church read a letter from his eldest daughter that sobered him up for the rest of his life.

Young Abby thought she'd had a dream that her sister kissed her.

Mr. Parker awoke brokenhearted having lost his son, his best driver, and his neighbor's daughter. Poor Kate was so distraught that she'd left town. He refused to cause further emotional harm and to be bitter. He stopped questioning the disappearance of Silas and instead focused on his business. He'd find in the rebuilding process that Peter McKendrick was not talented like his older brother and dismissed him.

Late in the day, after the fire had long expired, that steamer trunk was delivered by a two-seater buggy to a sprawling mansion in Alton. The receiver tipped the drivers well, and they drove off amazed at their fortune. In short order, Silas was headed through the remaining Underground to a sympathetic state further North where he found the aid to freedom he desperately needed. And Miss Katherine Church was asleep, clutching a case and satchel that held a sturdy bullwhip, on a steam train that roared into the sunset, bound for Iris, Texas.

Iris, Texas, 1895

This still feels like it happened yesterday.

Kate mused as she finished at the washstand, brushing her hands over the well-worn silk dressing gown. She petted Strax and glanced over the invitation one last moment before climbing into bed. She remembered Michael and sweetly caressed the whip wrapped on her bedpost. She missed him still, twenty years later. As Kate fell asleep, she decided to accept this invitation.

No use bemoaning old wounds. It was time to heal, time to move on.

8 A GENTLEMAN COMES

A gentleman had come to Iris on the noon train shortly after Riley's funeral. He wore similar clothes to the locals and followed a specific rule: "Do not draw attention to oneself." Gone was his formal top hat and tails. Despite his British ancestry, he didn't even bring a bowler. He wore a simple brown suit with a matching vest and a tan riverboat hat. He was in his late forties with pale blue-green eyes and well-groomed thinning brown hair that showed hints of gray. His matching mustache was trimmed and lay over a kind smile. He was over six feet and two inches tall, but of average build. He carried a brown leather case that held an interesting cache of items: non-descript clothing, money, papers, and weapons. He pulled a unique ornate pocket brass watch from his vest. It pulsed in his palm as he checked the time. This gentleman had several names at his disposal, but for now, he didn't require one.

Iris was a pass-through town, but the woman he was pursuing had been there for almost twenty years. *It must be quite the place to disappear*, he mused and scanned the rail platform. A couple of ranchers left the train and immediately departed to the general store for supplies. Other than folk running errands, the main street was quiet. The gentleman checked over the street then headed to the post and proffered a simple brown and twine-wrapped envelope to the postman. He in turn passed a map and other papers to the gentlemen, which he immediately tucked neatly into his case. No words between the two; just a nod of acceptance and the gentleman returned to the hot Texas sun.

The gentleman went round the back of the post to a waiting mustang and cart, loaded his case, and headed to a cabin far outside of Iris. Over the next week, he'd organized a plan and given a particular clergyman a donation in exchange for use of his collar, just for one day.

That day was a Sunday, a week after Mr. Riley's funeral. Bills at the post announced "no Mass due to illness," but visiting clergy was present to hear confessions at two p.m. And promptly at that time, Kate arrived at the church alone to unburden her soul.

"Father, forgive me for I have sinned," Kate began, her voice laced with sadness. She had waited patiently during the week to relieve the pain of having killed another soul. It stabbed at her heart like a hot poker. Her eyes were puffy from crying herself to sleep each night.

She was kneeling in the box of a confessional in the back of the church. On the other side of a dividing wall, scarcely visible through a petite opening, which was covered in a dark fabric screen, was an unusual priest. Unbeknownst to Kate, he wasn't a clergyman. This man wasn't part of Drasco's gang, a thief, or even a clever backward ranch hand.

Instead, the gentleman, adorned in the priest's collar, sat and listened intently. He spoke in a rich, lyrical voice. "Speak my child, tell me your sins," he intoned.

"Father, I shot and killed a man in a duel, and as a result of my actions, a man who was like my father was murdered." Kate shook and sobbed. "I shouldn't have done it and I am sorry." He felt her heart breaking and let her weep for a moment. He measured her reaction to killing.

Strax and the Widow

Was it brutal and how did she feel?

"Please tell me, my child. Did you initiate this or was this a sort of defense?" His tender words calmed Kate. She warmed to the visiting priest, forgot the danger she'd been in, and remembered only her own violence.

"I was defending guests in the saloon and was goaded by an evil man to participate. But it was my actions that caused the deaths." The gentleman liked this answer. It demonstrated responsibility and character.

He spoke kindly. "Dear child, we are given difficult choices. God gives us free will to carry out decisions, and at times we make mistakes. However, we are perfect in His eyes and that is why the Father offers us the opportunity to confess and do penance." The gentleman was bemused at his faux priestly wisdom.

Kate's heart slowed as she stopped crying. Her hands relaxed in meditation. She was relieved and silently wished that this clergyman was always here. "Thank you, Father, I am genuinely sorry for my sins." She spoke earnestly.

The gentleman was impressed with her sincerity. "You are forgiven, my child. But before your Act of Contrition, do you have any other sins to confess?"

Kate hesitated. A piece of her heart was still heavy. It might as well be now, she coached herself. "Father, I have had on occasion, impure thoughts and um, feelings about men."

The gentleman coughed loudly to cover his amusement at the unexpected admission.

He grinned to himself, desiring more details. "Please explain, my child. Remember, God is forgiving." He managed to get the words out without chuckling. *Contain yourself,* the gentleman reprimanded himself in a bemused fashion.

"Father, I have been alone for a long time," Kate stuttered, embarrassed. "I have no husband and I, uh, yearn to be with a man." To Kate, it was uncomfortably warm in the tiny confessional. She wiped her brow of sudden perspiration.

The gentleman's unseen smile grew, and he coughed again for a brief moment.

"Dear child, you have had relations with a man before?" the gentleman inquired. With his curiosity killing him, he had to test her experience. How could he use her? Could she fight a man? Could she flirt with or break one? He heard her frustrated sigh as the words fumbled out. He was subtle in his approach, but he was determined to know. "You mustn't be ashamed, child. God sees all, knows all." He again hid his mirth as he heard her deep exhale and she continued.

"Yes sir. I've been with a man." Kate remembered Michael Parker and relaxed. "But I loved him very, very much."

He felt the release of her tension with the sound of her gentle admission, not too brash, but not too cold.

"And you have confessed to this before and done penance?" he continued and demonstrated tremendous restraint despite his curiosity. Could she be honest? Would she follow thorough instructions? His mind reviewed the questions and answers. The gentleman was adept at his inquiries.

"Yes sir," she solemnly whispered.

"And you have not sinned since then?" he probed.

"No sir." Kate wondered when this confession would end. She'd done this before, she disliked the actual confession, but the emotional release afterward was an odd ecstasy.

The gentleman was covertly satisfied with her answers.

"Child, you should not be ashamed. Man was meant to be with woman, although God prefers that they be conjoined unto him and wedded. Continue to act like a lady in future endeavors; you are forgiven of your sins. Please say your Act of Contrition."

Kate was relieved; she refrained from revealing further details. She recited her Act.

The gentleman continued. "For your penance, please say one hundred Hail Marys and one hundred Our Fathers in the next twenty-four hours. You are absolved of all sins and may go." He delivered his orders with compassion and noted the sounds of Kate's relief.

"Thank you, Father," Kate retreated from confession and then left the church.

What the hell? Kate questioned herself as she mounted Sonny outside in the bright sunshine. How did this man of the cloth pull the truth out of her? She was comforted by his presence. Kate had confessed before, but he put her in a spell worthy of a wizard. She began her penance on the way home, but her mind whirled with what just happened.

It's been a rough week, she mused.

Once the gentleman heard the closing of the church door, he slid out of the confessional, gazed over the pews, and peeked outside to watch the woman leave. *She's a good one.* This is exactly why he came to Iris.

Over the next month, he observed her from afar, taking careful notes of her whereabouts. He'd received information that the rail office was closing even before Kate or Ferris were notified.

It was time to commence operations, he'd decided. *Now only if she agreed to participate*, the gentleman stewed. He'd sent the first invitation to the post. Now he awaited her reply.

9 A SWIM AND FRIENDLY GAMES OF POKER

The day after receiving the first invitation was a revelation. Kate felt a new purpose in life. She awakened to a mild rainstorm, but it was not a day to stay in bed despite the rail office now being closed on Saturdays. After taking Strax out, Kate went to the post in the general store at her normal noontime mail pick-up just as the train rolled away. The postman sorted the minuscule amount of mail and smiled briefly at her as she came in. Kate handed him the benefactor's card. Without a word, he handed her another similar mysterious package, along with a letter from home. Kate left and returned to her room to read both right away.

Kate opened the new invitation first as she had been paid to do it. It was the same paper, imprint, and lovely script:

"*Dear Miss Church:*

Thank you for accepting this first assignment. It is simple. There is a large stack of sacks behind the general store. Estimate the number of sacks; precision is not necessary at this time. Write only the number on the enclosed plain card. Do not address it to anyone. Please do this by Monday and return it to the postman during your usual noontime visit. The previous discretionary rules apply.

Your Benefactor,

W."

Kate trembled. She knew exactly of which sacks W spoke, the ones that held the odd powerful, liquid-filled tubes that people had died over. Her benefactor must know of them too. Kate was uneasy. She'd become involved in a world bigger than Iris. If W was truly from back east, obviously wealthy and well connected, he had serious interests in the liquid. And that mysterious concoction belonged to Drasco.

Shit, her heart pounded. *He knows. Perhaps it's for the better.*

Kate exhaled deeply and attempted to clear her mind. Perhaps she'd do this assignment and then just quit. If W paid her another hundred dollars, those funds would go a long way to getting her back home. Perhaps she'd up her play in poker before the rail office closed.

Kate needed to leave before the outpost met its demise, or she could meet hers. She and Ferris spent the weekdays packing and planning. Leaving early caused suspicion. Drasco's gang sought to silence them anyway. They went about their business discreetly, figuring out a way to get the remaining people out of town. But Kate was tired of acting like it was all pleasant; she hadn't stayed in Iris this long to be running scared. *Enough of this.* She stiffened and opened the letter from home.

The letter from her sister Abby only added to her anxiety.

Dearest Kate:

I must ask that you come home. Father has taken a sudden turn for the worse. He has been ill each day for a month now, sleeping most days and feeling tremendous amounts of pain that even opiates will not settle. Mr. Parker now visits daily with a doctor. He is uncertain how long Father will be with us still.

Mr. Parker went blind and sold his business. Martha is helping, but she too has aged and has become limited in her abilities.

Kate, I have no suitors and fear that I will be an old maid. The funds you have sent have been a Godsend supporting us all these years, but I don't know what we'll do without Daddy. Please hurry home if you can.

Your Sister,

Abby"

Oh no, now I have to leave, Kate fumed. She resisted the urge to tear the letter to shreds as her hands trembled. *Why did I stay away so long? How could I have been so selfish?*

The past haunted her for a moment as she remembered Michael Parker, the whipping, the fire, and running far, far away.

Twenty years, she reminisced sadly, her head down. It still seemed like yesterday.

Her father recovered enough to be in a wheelchair for several years, but a new pain in his back left him bedridden. Abby started writing letters for him as his illness increased. She was an adult now, twenty-six. Kate couldn't blame her for wanting a life for herself. And poor Martha, permanently separated from her only family. Even after all this time, Silas had never returned. Strax sensed her stress and whined. "It's okay, boy," she mumbled, failing to sound sweet to her trusty companion.

Her optimism from earlier in the day disappeared as Kate set the letters aside and turned back outside into the rain.

Kate counted the sacks. She had planned wisely, no one would be out in this weather to see her accomplish the task.

She moved behind the main street buildings to the backside of the general store. The sacks remained, although it was obvious some had been disturbed since the day Riley was murdered. Only seven remained. The tip of a bottle poked through the top of an opened sack. Obviously, Drasco didn't care about it being seen. But Kate was, and she discreetly returned to her room. Strax met her at the door, and she patted him on the head. She offed her wet coat and boots and sat on the bed to write.

Kate penned a letter to Abby, saying she'd be home soon and enclosed money. She wrote "seven" on the benefactor's card, and then stashed it with Abby's letter in her satchel. She read her Bible, then took Strax out for a brief walk. Kate desired to stay as close to her normal routine as possible. She continued to work for the benefactor. No matter what W's motives were, she needed his financial support.

Later, Kate went out for Saturday night poker for relief and to win. But it was a poor turnout—only two ranchers, Mr. Whitney, Ferris, and Kate. Ellie was bored and briefly pondered the idea of joining the game herself. She'd already sent the remaining two saloon girls upstairs with a snappy southern voice, "Go on up ladies. Not enough to entertain tonight." Even Strax was asleep at Kate's feet.

Mr. Whitney had been coming around still despite the lack of players. He was an attractive man in his mid-thirties, with coal-black hair and a beard. He dressed well for a traveling gambler, wearing matching suit coats and vests. He always had a pocket scarf at the ready. His attempts to flirt with Kate went unnoticed, or so he thought.

She'd all but ignored him to focus on the game, but in the back of her mind, she wondered why a man of his ilk was interested in her. Mr. Whitney was successful at winning the best pot of the night. The games were finished for the evening.

Ferris escorted a sullen Kate home. "It will be over soon, Kate. We'll get out of town without any trouble." Ferris assured her, but she was restless. "Have you planned for the end here?"

"Yes," she muttered. "I may have a couple of ideas. We have an escape in the dark the night before if we get everyone to leave at the same time. Heck can't be thirty left in town," she planned aloud. "And then we'd just leave on the noon train. They'd be watching."

"But they won't just let you go, will they Kate?" Ferris fretted.

"I'm afraid you're right. Drasco wants something from me, but I have no idea what. Maybe he's just a sadist, toying with me. He hasn't been back, at least not during daylight hours." Kate purposely withheld information. Drasco was at least moving the dangerous liquids for a nefarious reason.

"Kate, I'd do whatever it took to protect you," Ferris said confidently. He squeezed her hand tightly. The walk from the saloon to her stairs had been far too short for him.

Kate sighed. She sensed that he still longed for more than her friendship.

"Ferris, I'd welcome that support, but I'll be alright." She gracefully declined. "You be ready when we get our plan together. Goodnight."

"Goodnight, Kate." Ferris went home to the hotel.

Kate and Strax went to her room, and she relaxed. *Maybe they'd all leave at once*, she thought to herself as she fell into a restless slumber.

Sunday dawned sunny and hot. Kate spent the day with Chin and Ming. They took a clothed swim in the creek, laughing and splashing like children. Their fun was interrupted by a cry just a stone's throw away. "Miss Kate, you hear?" Ming panicked.

"Yes, shhh," Kate whispered, and they halted. It happened again, this time with a wail. Kate motioned and they eased down the creek bed, sloshing through the shallow water. They turned around past their tent to see a native toddler, naked and muddy, having just slid down the steep bank. He was tangled in a fallen tree and the thick silt.

"Oh, baby!" Ming exclaimed and the trio rushed forward, pulling him out. Ming wiped him down in the cool water, causing the child to giggle cheerfully.

Chin spoke softly. "How did child get here?"

They laughed with the now bemused child.

But another sound was heard. High on the bank bluff were deep voices speaking in an unfamiliar tongue. The trio paused and peeked up to see a half dozen Indians, including a female that was extremely upset. The braves were stone-faced, staring down. *Oh no*, Kate panicked, *we have their baby.*

They froze.

Kate bolstered herself, *Keep calm*. The hairs on the back of her neck stood on end as she crept towards Ming.

"Ming, give me the child," Kate whispered as her skin crawled with tension.

"Miss Kate..." Ming quivered.

"Ming, shhh, just hand him to me." Kate took the child and began to walk to the bank, never losing eye contact with the natives. She prayed that they'd be peaceful. "They'd like him back."

She was right; the six were motionless as Kate stuck the path and carried the still smiling toddler to the upset native woman. "Here," she whispered. The female cried sweetly and took the child to her bosom. Kate backed away, rejoining her friends in the water. The braves assisted the mother onto a horse as she cooed to her baby. They then rode off in silence. Even their horses tread lightly on the desert floor. Kate exhaled. She had never seen so many natives up close.

"You're kind, Miss Kate." Ming hugged Kate tightly and Chin touched her back. "Strong mark, see it protect you!" And Ming poked her now old tattoo.

Kate chuckled in agreement. "Yes, I am strong now."

The kind group dried off on the bank of the creek as they shared stories. Kate brought them supplies, and they enjoyed a late supper as the sun set. Ming and Chin welcomed the supplies. They were cleaning at the hotel or saloon when there wasn't much left to do.

The Chinese couple had lived such a hard life. Ming was the daughter of one of the last samurai. She'd disobeyed an emperor to marry Chin. Coming to America had not been easy. They'd never had material things, but they always had each other.

At least running worked for someone, Kate mused as she turned for home that evening. She resolved to herself again, that it was time to go home.

On Monday she mailed Abby's letter and returned the benefactor's card. The postman handed her a packet stuffed with another hundred dollars and a letter.

"Dear Miss Church:

Thank you for your service. Additional opportunities will be available, and I will contact you in a similar fashion. As always please follow these strict guidelines:

-Dress and act like a lady.

-Do not draw attention to yourself.

-Complete each task as requested and on time.

-Be prompt but do not act in haste.

-Show no emotion in completing tasks.

-Do not question any instruction or giver or receiver of information.

-Never look back after a meeting is finished or a task is completed.

-Avoid violence unless your own life is in danger.

I will be in contact soon.

Your Benefactor,

W."

Kate pursed her lips at the serious tone of this latest letter. How soon before another assignment was made? Would it be in time for her to receive more payments before having to leave?

Kate didn't have to wait long. Her mind had been clouded. But her benefactor had her best interests at heart. Work was indeed available.

The invitations were coming regularly, about every other day. It was the same situation each time. Tobias seemed to appear out of nowhere, pulled her sleeve, and handed her the latest invite. It was sealed with a capital "W" imprinted in red wax. Kate completed whatever was required and cash arrived at the post. Some duties were simple—to write down the address of a building along the main street or count how many ranchers arrived on a particular date. Others were complicated, such as *"Snatch one of the sacks and give it to the coachman on the noontime train."*

The benefactor was collecting information: who knew whom, the number of men possibly with Mr. Drasco, was the train ever late, and when were deliveries made to the saloon and general store?

Kate realized that she was completing serious business indeed when W asked her to investigate an empty building across from the saloon. The invitation came from Tobias as usual. He came over to the rail office late in the afternoon as she was cleaning up. He always made sure that she was alone, Tobias following instructions from the postman.

"Thanks, Miss Kate!" Tobias trotted off with a tip.

Kate pretended to be filling her satchel, but she deftly opened and read the letter under the cover of the well-worn leather bag:

Dear Miss Church:

I need you to investigate a particular building. It is the grey one, directly across from the saloon. You probably know that it has been vacated for well over a year now. Please report what's inside, how much, etc.? Do not enter unless necessary.

Your Benefactor,

W.

However, when Kate peered in a few hours later, when most of the town had gone home for the day, it was far from vacant. The warehouse was filled to the rafters with crates and sacks of the powerful green liquid-filled tubes.

Uh-oh. This is troubling. She tried not to worry about it and focus on the money she was making.

Kate did as she was told and did not question. She simply observed or completed each assignment, wrote the answers on the usual card, and gave it to the postman, marked only with "W." She adhered strictly to the benefactor's rules, she did not ask the postman any questions. She did not speak, but only to request the mail or see if any parcels had been delivered. She acted like a lady and showed no emotion whatsoever at the post. She was on time, not hurried, and completed her jobs efficiently. Most of all, she never looked back at the post once she'd left, no matter what the situation.

This discipline was profitable. Kate had enough to return home and buy into a poker game before the office closed. What saddened her was that she hid this new venture from Ferris. He was just as lost as she was. The final days at the rail office were painful. The silence was deafening. He'd wired and written several employers back East but had yet to find employment.

Kate sensed Ferris' desire, but she just didn't have a romantic interest in him. Ferris deserved to be with a grounded, genteel lady.

Her focus was on completing the tasks and leaving…alone. Kate realized she couldn't save the whole town. To pass the time, they discussed the upcoming final game of poker and the possibility of winning enough for a safe exit.

Maybe they'd bribe their way out, Kate wondered.

Ellie promoted that poker game and even hired a desperate soul to post signs in a couple of neighboring towns. She'd have to abandon the saloon if there weren't enough visitors.

That night in the saloon was its last hurrah. Ellie had drawn in ranchers, Mr. Whitney, and travelers including a new player—Mr. King—and unfortunately Drasco and his gang. They'd managed to stay undercover, but this evening, they apparently felt invited back to the saloon. The ruthless cowpokes had arrived late after the games began at seven. The players paused for a moment as they joined the others. Ellie bit her lip as the tension-filled the room, but she waved them in.

Ferris inhaled as if to speak up, but Kate touched his leg and whispered "No." Ferris snarled as the current hand finished and Drasco and his gang were dealt in.

Ellie brought over drinks. "Five-card draw gentlemen and…lady." She winked at Kate. "Twenty-five dollars buy-in." The players groaned and whistled. Kate slid money under the table to a stunned Ferris.

"Where'd you get this?" he inquired, leaning to her.

"Never mind, pay attention." Kate was ready, her swagger was back. Strax, her ever-ready good luck charm, rested at her side. The first hands were brutal for the lesser gamblers.

After the first hour, the groups went from six to two as player after player ran out. By nine p.m., it was a single table with four players left: Drasco, Mr. Whitney, Mr. King, and Kate. Members of Drasco's gang and Ferris had stayed to watch the hands unfold. Cigar smoke circled the players as the bets went higher and the bluffs harder to read. Ellie swore she'd never heard the words "I'll raise you" so much in her life. Initially, the wins were easy—two pair, three of a kind. But other successes made the players suspicious as if one had packed an extra deck in their pocket.

"Full house." Kate dropped down two queens and a trio of tens. As she dragged in over seven hundred in chips, the men moaned.

"Shit! Ellie, drink!" Drasco commanded and disappointedly lit another cigar. The saloon owner brought a fresh round of whiskey to the competitive clan.

Mr. Whitney also seemed unhappy, although several times he tried to slip a hand under to graze Kate's leg. But a growl from Strax and his embarrassment at the table's laughter stopped that nonsense. "Better stop trying to pet that dog or are you hoping to get that pussy?" Drasco hollered and his watchful gang chortled.

Mr. King was a harder read. He didn't say a lot but earned enough wins to keep him in the game. He was steady and serious, nattily dressed in brown with his intense blue-green eyes shaded by a boater. The saloon girls stood by him all evening, but not once was he distracted. He didn't have a tell either, but Kate noticed he watched how she played. *Was he letting her win?* she wondered.

Indeed, he was. Mr. King was a gentleman; at least that was his plan today. His motives were not to win but to observe and perhaps support Miss Church.

Kate shook off the negativity and refocused. Mr. Whitney won the next hand, although it was a lesser pot of seventy-five.

Drasco twittered, "So you aren't interested in getting in Miss Katie's bloomers."

Kate ignored him as the next hand was dealt. Initially, the wins were evenly distributed, but then it turned into an incredible evening for Kate as she won the next five hands. On the last win, she'd drawn a high straight outright; ten, Jack, Queen, King, and Ace. The men groaned. Drasco was out and on his way to a drunken stupor. The saloon clock chimed midnight.

"Alright, time's up!" Ellie shouted happily, relieved she'd sold more cigars and whisky that night than she had in months. "Now I can dump this joint," she muttered under her breath while clearing the table. Drasco seemed ready to protest but backed away.

"Well boys, seems like it's time to head out." He leaned toward his remaining gang, and they left without issue. Mr. King tipped his hat and eased into the cool darkness outside.

Did they let me win?

As Kate was distracted, Mr. Whitney leaned in a bit too close. He disrupted her with a drunken, dirty whisper, "That'll get you a lot of fine things. Why don't we split it, then I'll split you open?"

Strax sat up and growled.

The flirty gambler slid back and winked.

"No thank you, Mr. Whitney. Goodnight." Kate spoke firmly. Ferris glared disgustedly at Mr. Whitney as he departed. The remaining folks happily stood around Kate.

"Kate, you're amazing!" Ferris laughed as she stacked up several thousands of dollars.

"You fooled those boys from round one." Ellie laughed. "Don't spend it all here."

"Here, you earned this." Kate tipped her hostess a stack of bills close to a hundred dollars.

Ellie leaned in and touched her hand. "Be careful, Kate. Put that to good use and get your ass outta here, and quick."

"I will," Kate whispered, "don't worry." Ferris took her arm and they strolled out as Ellie shut down the saloon.

"Okay, what are you planning?" he inquired the moment they hit the street. Strax scampered along happily, sensing his master's fortune.

"I have an idea, but I have to flesh it out." Kate was still stunned at her winnings. Money changed a lot. It had bought Silas freedom, she remembered. Maybe it could do the same for the remaining residents of Iris. "I'm sending funds home. My father is unwell."

"Aren't you going home, Kate? When the office closes?" Ferris was perplexed.

"Well, yes, but…who knows what might happen." Her voice trailed for a moment, but she pulled herself together. "Ferris don't be such a worrywart. Go home." She encouraged her friend. She was truly encouraged for the first time in months.

"Goodnight, Kate." He smiled somberly as he left.

"Goodnight, Ferris. C'mon, Strax." She collected her other best friend.

As they climbed the stairs to the room, the visiting gentleman who heard Kate's confession just a few weeks ago, now watched her go up from the darkness. He checked his pocket watch. He was concerned at the turn of the evening's events. Mr. Whitney teased her and Drasco had ulterior motives.

It was time to bring her in before she got hurt, the wise gentleman plotted.

But he wasn't the only one watching Kate that late evening. Before the gentleman stopped by, another visitor had come and left just as quickly.

As Kate walked in the door, she stepped on a folded piece of paper. She didn't dare light a lantern. Instead, she shut her door, ordered Strax to stay, and picked up the letter. In the near darkness she read the note:

"Miss Church:

There is an urgent matter. Meet me tomorrow, high noon near the church after Mass."

Her mind raced. Should she meet W? She had all the necessities now. But he promised employment that better guaranteed her future. Kate stashed the money in her satchel, undressed, and slid into bed. Strax curled up below her feet and fell asleep long before his master. She'd decide tomorrow. The deadline to leave was closing. Kate had a couple of days to piece together a plan.

10 INTERVENTION

Kate awoke for the second time that Sunday with a clear sun in her eyes, but her mind was murky. She blinked. Her mouth was dry with a peculiar taste.

The first time she'd awakened that morning, Kate dressed, grabbed her satchel, and rode Sonny out to the church. Kate dismounted and tied him outside the empty building. Oddly, Mass wasn't held that day, not a soul in sight. But someone was lurking. The last thing Kate felt at the church was a gloved hand covering her mouth.

As Kate gained lucidity, she realized she'd been ambushed and drugged. The note wasn't from the benefactor.

How could I have been so stupid? I even left without my gun and whip.

The paper wasn't the parchment, there wasn't a seal, and it wasn't even signed with the flourish of a "W."

Kate was coming round and attempting to stand when she heard him, the gravelly-voiced demon, Drasco. His shadow cast over her, way too close for comfort. "Well now, she's comin' round, a cheatin' bitch," he bellowed. "Taking our big bills, boys." He glanced back at five of his men. "Yeah, cheating at poker isn't right in this town. You'll never cheat again. We'll make certain of it." He grinned wickedly.

Kate realized she was having trouble getting up because her hands were tied, the thick rope digging into her skin. *Oh no.* She recalled the night that the barn was destroyed by McKendrick in St. Louis and shuddered. The flashback made her seethe with anger.

Think! She assessed the situation, six of them and several horses. Sonny was nowhere in sight. Worst of all, the rope that held her hands was tied to a tamed mustang. "I didn't cheat," she stuttered and gathered her courage. "I played fair and square."

"Well, you lost your money any way you little hussy, looky here." He cackled as he held up her satchel with the previous night's winnings. "You won't be needing this anyhow." He threw it to a gang member who hung it on his saddle horn.

Kate trembled. It was all going downhill in a flash.

"Tell me, Katie, why ain't you like the dancing girls? You're a woman, aren't you? Heh." His cackling made her head ache.

Kate felt a raw pit in her stomach, that overwhelming sense that this was terribly wrong. This might be her final moment; a painful, tragic end. But this time she'd fight. "I am a lady," she spoke, this time with solid confidence.

"Boys, we should take a peek for ourselves!" He lurched forward, clenched her tied wrists, and yanked her up flush to his body. He smelled of dust and whisky. "C'mon, let's have fun, darling!" He grabbed her, forced a kiss, and pushed her right back.

Kate wavered, still lightheaded. His beard was rough and made her lips bleed.

"Ha, she tastes good, boys. I'm gonna have more of this," he growled and jerked her forward.

This time Kate was ready. She vehemently spat in his eyes and drove a furious boot into his shin.

"Oowww, bitch!" Drasco yelled and slapped her.

But Kate stood solid. She heard Chin's stoic voice in her head, "You are strong now." Blood trickled from her mouth, and she craned her neck to wipe it on her shoulder as her hands were still tied.

She was grabbed round from behind and lifted. "I got her, boss," one cowboy yelled. "I wanna piece." He salivated in her ear.

Kate dug a boot heel in his shin, scraped it down the nerve line to his ankle and he dropped her on all fours.

A third outlaw kicked her ribs, and then her buttocks. She fell face-first in the dirt, their evil laughter rattling in her brain. Kate struggled to get up, sputtering dirt from her lips.

"Haw, now that's a reason to spit." Drasco laughed. "Well, now if you ain't cooperating, we should just get down to business. We didn't bring you out here for nothing," the gang leader growled. "We have a deal for you missy. I know you'll be outta a job and you have skills with shootin.' Heck, you're one of the best poker cheats I've ever seen. You can join us, and we can put those talents to use. You just gotta be willing to give us some pussy." The gang hooted and snickered at Drasco's offer.

"No," Kate wheezed the word out.

"What's that?" He laughed over her and squeezed her fanny. "I bet it'd be nice seeing your arse from behind while I fuck it."

Kate felt a reserve of strength and managed to crawl. "No!" she repeated loud enough that her ears rang.

The cowboy's laughter burned her pride.

Dirt still covered her eyes, and she shook it out. Kate heard one of the men mount a horse. *No, no, this cannot happen.* She felt the rope tug and her vision cleared.

Drasco bent down to her and teased, "Well missy, I give you one more chance. You can play along with us, and I'll let you live, hmmm?"

"No," she whispered, her parched throat stifling her voice.

"What's that?" he drawled.

"I said no." She coughed.

Drasco whistled to his cohort on the horse. He slapped the reigns, and the mustang began to move forward. After only seconds, the rope tightened and took Kate with it.

They are dragging the dignity out of me, she feared. The rocky dirt of the desert scraped through her blouse and scarred her elbows. She tucked her chin in her shoulder as she bounced along. They whooped as the rider stopped and then started. Dirt caked her body and poured into her corset. Her eyes welled up into her sleeve. *No, don't get upset, no emotion, remember the rules,* she resolved.

They stopped. An eerie silence, then the thunder of horses caused Kate to peek up.

A tribe of natives arriving. Oh, Jesus, could this get any worse? Kate internally begged for mercy as a tribe arrived. *Please just be quick, God.*

Drasco threw up his hands in a flurry. "Well, we don't want no trouble here." His gang was surrounded and outnumbered. The natives stared them down as Kate rolled over onto her bottom. A sense of relief rose as she recognized the young native mother with her rescued child tied securely in a papoose on her back. He cooed at her. Kate returned a dusty grin.

Without a word, the native chief dismounted, pulled a tomahawk from his belt, and chopped the rope that drug Kate through the dusty desert. Kate looked at the natives, then the gang.

Begrudgingly, Drasco motioned to his men. "Alrighty then, we'll just make our way out."

The chief made a low moan and pointed at Kate's satchel still tied to the cowboy's saddle. That rider trembled as he loosened the stolen satchel and tossed it back to Kate.

Only then did a couple of the natives pull their horses aside and let the wretched gang leave. As they made their way further into the distance, Kate saw the dirt kick up from their horses as they gained speed. They wouldn't be coming back today. One of the braves cut her hands free and helped her stand. She gazed directly into his eyes, spoke a quiet "Thank you," and nodded to the others. Kate heard another horse and turned to see another member of the tribe leading Sonny to her. They helped her mount as not another word was spoken. The chief pointed and the tribe galloped away with the braves whooping loudly.

Kate turned around with wide eyes, stunned at the miraculous chain of events, and saw the steeple of the church peeking over a ridge. And out of the corner of her eye, she spied an odd blue-green cactus glistening in the sun.

Although Kate ached, she approached the peculiar plant. It was oozing the powerful green liquid. Hundreds of the same cacti behind it glistened. Kate laughed at her fortune. That's why they'd brought her here; they were collecting from the plants. Drasco pushed to change her, lure her into their gang, and force her to show them how she was using the cacti. They'd failed.

Despite her improved mood, Kate couldn't return to town in the shape she was in. She patted Sonny's mane and headed for Ming and Chin's tent.

11 BRANDED

Something was amiss long before Kate arrived at Ming and Chin's tent. A thin tendril of gray smoke rose just over the bank of the creek in the distance as she approached. "C'mon Sonny!" she urged, slapped the reins, and hurried the horse into a full gallop. It was mid-afternoon; they wouldn't be cooking. As she closed in, a burning smell assaulted her nostrils. It was not food, and the haze was thicker. She guided Sonny onto the creek bed path towards her friends' home.

When Kate rounded the bend, her heart stopped. She completely forgot her pain. Ming and Chin were sprawled out in front of their tent, or what was left of it. Smoldering pieces were still burning in the hot sun.

"Nooooo!" Kate's scream echoed off the creek's muddy cliffs. "Oh God, oh no. Please no." Kate nearly fell from dismounting too fast. She stumbled to her friends in a panic. She shook Ming's lifeless body and pushed her hair aside. Her eyes were glazed over, and a nasty white froth trickled from her mouth. Kate inhaled as she fell back in shock. Ming's body was already cold, even in the warm sun.

Kate crawled to Chin and began to weep. He too had the same foam dripping from his lips; they were poisoned. He was bloody; he'd protected his wife, Kate grimaced. She frantically checked over his body to find Drasco's burn mark. He branded

Chin's buttocks so hard it burnt through his clothes and seared his skin. They did the same to Ming, only they ripped her dress and pulled her bloomers down to get to bare skin.

"Fucking heartless bastards; no dignity whatsoever!" Kate hollered and kicked aside some of the crispy embers. Drasco's gang left her a violent warning before Kate tussled with them, as if she hadn't had enough deviance for the day. She collapsed into a heap on the bank with a violent cry racking her soul.

After a few moments of complete despair, Kate heard Chin's voice in her head, "You strong now." She stood, steadied herself, and checked her surroundings cautiously. *Gather your wits, show no emotion.* Kate homed in on her strengths. She gathered Ming's clothes together and with a swipe of her palm closed Ming's eyes that had been frozen in terror. Kate despised the thought that the last people Ming saw were her killers. "Fuck them. Oh, Ming, you deserved so much better than this."

She wrapped both bodies in Sonny's horse blanket, put them as close as possible to the lingering fire, and set them ablaze. "Ashes to ashes, dust to dust, dust you are and to dust you shall return. Thank you, Ming, thank you, Chin. My gratitude is without end." At the same time, another fire was lit; a passionate resolve of revenge rose in Kate's belly.

This will not end well for Drasco, Kate promised herself as the fire finally died out. She dug a pit near the water line and buried as much of the ash as she could carry, then brushed away the remainder into the flow.

Her body ached as she dipped into the creek and cleaned her clothes. She took her time and let the sun dry her until it hung low in the autumn sky. She braided her hair neatly and did her best to hide the tearing of her clothes. All the while, anger and revenge propelled her forward. By twilight, she'd returned to town and tied Sonny up behind the hotel.

In the dusk, she slid through the back door of the empty hotel kitchen and went up to Ferris's room. Seeing light under the door, she rapped on it. He peeped out and upon seeing Kate, waved her in.

"My God, what happened?" Ferris exclaimed.

Oh, shit, Kate mused to herself, *I must be beat up.*

Ferris dipped a cloth in his washbasin and dabbed Kate's swollen lips.

She leaned towards the basin's mirror to see her bruised visage.

"Kate, are you okay?"

"Yes, yes." She turned away from the mirror.

"Here, sit. Water?" He led her to his bed and poured a glass before she responded. He drew his curtains, then sat beside her as she drank.

"It was Drasco. They ambushed me, out by the church." Kate realized she should remain silent about the invitations and her benefactor. "I'd gone to church, and they were waiting for me." She fibbed and then laughed as Ferris seemed confused at her amusement. "They were going to kill me, but I was rescued by Indians."

"What? Kate, no, truly?"

"Yes—" And then, like an insane person, her laughter turned to sobs and she whispered, "They killed Ming and Chin." Ferris pulled her close as she wiped her eyes and continued,

"Which is why I came straight here. Ferris, do me a favor and not question it." Kate was deadly serious. Ferris hardly believed what he'd just heard.

"Of course, anything." He was eager to hear her thoughts considering her day's misadventure.

"You have to leave tomorrow, go to St. Louis, and marry my sister Abby." His mouth fell wide open. "Please, I know this is a strange arrangement. But I know that you will care for her. I have enough winnings to help you get started, a substantial dowry."

"Kate, I don't know. I am stunned." He was ghostly pale, but his eyes twinkled.

She took his hand. "Ferris, I know that you have always liked me, but I just, I'm not meant for the kind of life you have in mind. Abby will appreciate a man like you." Kate was somber for her friend.

Ferris cared for his broken cohort. "Kate, what about you? The office isn't closing for another day."

"Anyone who has bothered to stay knows that we're leaving anyway. We'll post it tomorrow at the station and leave notes for those that are left, twenty altogether." Ferris saw a plan in her eyes. "They'll leave, I know they will. You must go at noon tomorrow. They're working their way down to me and now you're in their way. You must promise me you'll leave and not look back. I can't tell you much else." Kate had enough resources to bribe whoever was left in town to get out. She would stuff the notes to the remaining residents with cash. She was confident her plan to desert the town would be implemented. *Why do I have to be so damned responsible?* She derided herself for a moment then remembered her promise to Riley.

"Alright then." Ferris interrupted. "I'll go, but what can I do to help now?"

"I'd wondered when you were going to ask." She twittered and then winced at her fat lip. "We're headed to the office now. Give me your clothes." Ferris stuffed a couple of suits in a sack and the two-headed into the cool darkness for the empty rail office.

They went around the back to the tool shed and only then did they procure a low lamp. Once inside, Ferris was amazed at the sight of the contraptions Kate put together. "What is this?"

"It's our distraction, a way out. Carry these into the office." She handed him a set of pulleys, ropes, tools, and odd items. They peered round and headed inside the lowly building. Kate instructed her manager on the setup of their farce. They attached wheels to the chairs and mounted the pulleys to the walls. The ropes were laced together and tied to hitches in a box containing an intricate series of cogs, wires, and a dismantled clock that was happily ticking away. "Okay, now the clothes you brought. And turn around, no peeking."

"What?"

"I said, don't peek." Kate undressed as Ferris blushed, staring out the window. She put on a set of his clothing. "Okay, turn around. This is interesting." She laughed.

He turned to see Kate in his rumpled suit, smiling like a happy child. "Now what?" He laughed. She opened a cabinet and gathered several stacks of rags she saved for this occasion. Kate rolled several into two round head shapes.

"Okay, the other set of your clothes. Stuff them with these and set them in your chair. Pass your hat too."

"We're making dummies?" he mused incredulously.

"Oh yes." Kate stuffed her beaten duds she just offed. They mounted their lookalikes onto the office chairs, placed their hats, and Kate wound a crank on her box invention. The ropes pulled the chairs back and forth. The glow from the lamp illuminated the now animated imposters. Ferris felt like he had walked into a Christmas play.

"Kate, you're spectacular!" he exclaimed. "Will it keep going?"

"It should. I've tested it in the shed. It's self-winding. It'll run until it either the cogs dry out or the ropes wear down, which should give us plenty of time to fool the nasty fellows." Kate admired her achievement. "Alright then, a short office closing note on the door and we're out of here." They both checked the room for a moment. The wheels made a low hum as they rolled across the now worn floorboards. Ferris took her hand.

"You're absolutely wonderful, Kate. You look fine in that suit of mine." He kissed her cheek and she blushed.

"You are too. I wouldn't trust my sister with anyone else. We must get back and pack for tomorrow." They posted the note on the office door, worded "Rail Office Closing tomorrow. Please do not disturb." Of course, she counted on Drasco ignoring the post and peeking in the curtains. They were left open just wide enough that two figures could be seen moving inside. It should buy them time to escape.

They stole back to the hotel. As Ferris packed a single bag, Kate penned a letter to Abby. Only it wouldn't be delivered by post. Ferris was prepared to use it as his introduction to the Church family. Kate took a stack of bills from her satchel.

"Oh Kate, my God." Ferris's eyes were wide. "I can't."

"You must, you promised. Remember?" She choked. "Now tomorrow, leave out the backside of the hotel at the last possible moment for the noon train. Speak to no one."

"Kate, you will leave, won't you?" he stuttered.

"Yes, but I can't tell you how." Kate swallowed a hard lump in her throat. "Please, just love my sister as if you would've loved me."

"I promise Kate. Take care. I will see you soon."

"Thank you, Ferris." They hugged warmly and Kate slipped out into the night. It was midnight and a full moon had risen in the Texas sky.

What a rotten day. Kate trudged past the saloon, leading Sonny along. It was dark. *Ellie must've decided not to open the bar. Why even bother, she must've reasoned. Hopefully, she left,* Kate prayed.

She passed round the side of the building to her stairs. At the bottom, a large lump was lit by moonlight. As Kate approached, her eyes adjusted to another terror. Her beloved Strax was motionless. "Strax," she whispered. "Strax, boy, c'mon now." Sonny whinnied as she tied him to the stair rail. "Strax?" Still no motion. After checking around, she knelt next to her passed companion. Kate felt his silky fur near the neck. His body stiffened in the cool air. Her eyes filled with tears, as she stroked the back of her most faithful friend. She bit her swollen lip so as not to bawl aloud.

Bastards, her mind screamed. She had to withhold any visual anger. Her plan had to be implemented without causing notice.

Surveying the ground, she saw a piece of meat near his mouth, and just like Ming and Chin, a white foam glistened from his tongue and a dark patch of branded fur interrupted his white silken coat. "I am sorry my friend—my baby." She cooed and patted him. "You deserved more than I gave you. But I promise you," she whispered in his cone ear, "they will pay for what they have done." Kate wrapped her murdered friend in Ferris's suit coat and buried him in the ash pit behind the saloon. She was now thoroughly exhausted. Her legs ached with each movement as she climbed the stairs.

Kate checked her room without turning on a lamp. They jimmied the lock but only to get Strax. Nothing else had been touched. Drasco left her several violent messages that day and she had painfully received them.

She fell into bed fully clothed, her pistol and whip in hand. She clutched her pillow and screamed her withheld agony, letting her tears and anger out at last.

They're gonna pay and it'll be without mercy she vowed as a fitful sleep came over her.

Across the street, in the dark, the gentleman checked his pocket watch. It was time. Tomorrow was the most important day of their lives.

12 BOOM

Kate awoke abruptly. She sat up, her breathing labored. Each inhale painfully pressed her bruised ribs. *Did that really happen? Or was it a cruel, long nightmare?* Feeling Ferris's woolen suit on her body confirmed that the previous day's events were indeed real. Her hands clamped around her weaponry as she'd slept. Fortunately, she wasn't forced to use it.

She stretched and swung her legs over the side of the bed. Out of habit, Kate reached down for Strax at his favorite place at the foot of the bed, but only empty air. It had been a horrible day. "One more day of hell." She sighed as the sun rose over Iris.

Her body was pitifully sore, and she wore the bruises and scrapes to match. She'd tend to them later. She only wet her cheeks to wake. The last of her work to be done. Kate took out the remainder of her parchment and wrote out eleven short notes, each with the same simple message:

"Please leave town by tomorrow. There will be no one left to protect you."

She tucked the letters into envelopes filled with cash and addressed each to the families or persons left, ones that'd leave if they only had the means. Kate was giving them their chance.

She smoothed Ferris's suit over her body and pulled on one of her gambler hats. If anyone was watching, they wouldn't expect her in this costume. And they'd be unpleasantly surprised that she possessed Riley's shotgun, her whip, and a pistol tucked in the baggy pants. They were a perfect fit for this trip. Kate smiled to herself. She tucked the letters in with her cache of defense and left for the post.

Kate checked out the deserted and appropriately silent street for special delivery. She slid so swiftly down that Sonny didn't even stir. The post opened at nine a.m. The letters had to be ready for the noon mail drop from the train. Most in town still came to the post at noon. She was counting on the decent residents to keep up their daily habits despite Iris's downfall.

She walked briskly to the post under a crisp blue sky. The postman was turning the sign to "Open" just as she approached. Kate waltzed in and pretended to check out the remaining general store supplies as the postman opened his desk. She walked to the counter and stared straight at her contact.

He looked over his spectacles and rolled up his sleeves.

Kate only smiled expectantly.

He sighed. "Ma'am, er, um, Sir, I have no letters or packages today."

"I know, I have a delivery."

"I was not anticipating a package from you at this early hour." He was stern. *She should not be here and why on earth is she in a man's clothing?* He tried to control his toes from tapping.

"I will be clear, then." Kate's voice rose. "These letters are to be given to their addressees today. No exceptions." She whipped out the letters from the loose trousers and set them on the counter with unwavering determination.

The postman ran his hand through his short-cropped, dark thinning hair and twirled his handlebar mustache anxiously. "You do know that tomorrow is the final day for both the post and the rail? I can't be responsible for any mail unclaimed after that," he drawled.

Damn that contact, he flustered. Any break in his instruction might mean death. He'd better have that ride ready out of town tomorrow, the postman mused. He wouldn't be here to help Miss Church and he sure as hell didn't want to be left here after closing tomorrow.

"Understood. Do the best you can for our situation. You know what to do with any leftover mail. Thank you, sir." Kate turned and began to leave.

"Godspeed, Miss Church. Don't be too hard," the postman whispered. Kate left without looking back. The postman gazed at the letters, and it was just as he surmised; one for each of the remaining folks in Iris. *Damn, did she have to warn them? Aw hell. The town would be dead tomorrow. Any man who stayed was a fool.*

He peered out the window for a moment then reached under the counter for a package that just arrived. He had his instructions, a map, and supplies from the gentleman. He too was leaving for broader horizons.

Kate pulled down her welding goggles as the sun seemed brighter in the autumn sky. Or maybe it was her head that still ached from the conflicts causing her to squint. Still, no sign of anyone in the street. She peered around and then hurried back to the saloon. She stole to the side, fed Sonny, got fresh water, and then dashed up to her room to watch the fruits of her labor and generosity. It was only 9:30 a.m.

"The waiting is the hardest part now," she mumbled as the sun inched its way towards noon. She poured fresh water into the basin and properly cleaned up. Kate put a cool damp cloth on her forehead to calm her skin and then applied makeup that the saloon girls gave her. It covered the mess well. She stashed apples, bread, and jerky to eat as she sat on a stool to peek out the window and waited for an exodus to begin.

Promptly at 11:45 a.m., Ferris left payment for the hotel under the door of the room he stayed in for his long term in Iris. He didn't risk leaving from the front desk.

The night before, he'd wisely slept in a different room down the hall. He'd heard footsteps late in the eve, walking in his old doorway and right back out. If they'd looked in, they'd found an empty room, he felt confident in his cleverness. They'd assume he'd checked out.

He was correct. The gang headed for the rail office after sunrise. It was several hours before they realized it wasn't Kate and Ferris in the office, but a set of stuffed imposters.

Ferris parted from the deserted kitchen where Kate snuck in the night before. He was deliberate in his walk to the post. The general store portion had closed and now the post was the bastion of rail tickets. And there'd be a run on them later that day. Ferris slid into the post and requested politely. "A ticket to St. Louis, please."

The postman acted as if he knew this was where it was all going to hell. "Yes sir, one way?"

"Yes please." The postman pulled out the packet of tickets, filled out his papers, and gave the rail manager his ride out of Iris. What Ferris hadn't seen under the counter was a separate set of tickets and a revolver. After Kate left, the postman prefilled a ticket for each letter. He'd only put down a destination and date in order to get the hell out of Iris if all went sour.

"Thank you, sir, keep the change." Ferris left for the station. He was the only person on the platform as the train churned into Iris with minutes to spare before noon.

The conductor returned from a mail drop to the post, took his ticket uneventfully, and shouted "All aboard!" Ferris sighed as he jumped into the car. Passengers were seated, none suspicious in appearance. As he took his seat and the train whistle signaled its departure, Ferris silently wished for Kate's safety.

Meanwhile, Kate saw her future brother-in-law discreetly cross the street.

Perfect, no problems, or so she thought.

A few were heading for the post to pick up mail, just as planned. But from the corner of her eye, Kate saw Tobias fitfully pacing just outside the saloon. Oh no, she hadn't heard from W. in days and her tiny messenger held an invitation. She jumped up and bolted down to her petite contact.

"Miss Kate, oh, Miss Kate." Tobias was crying as she came to him. Then she heard it, the unmistakable cackle of a devil on earth.

"Well now, seems the boy has a gift for you. Better be careful!" Drasco drawled. He was only yards away, on a horse with two men behind him. Kate grabbed her pistol, but instead of drawing, the gang took off laughing. In the distance, she heard the train coming.

She kneeled and put her hand on the shoulder of her friend who was shaking with sobs. "Tobias, what is it?" He passed her the note with a trembling hand. Kate unfolded it to see a single word,

"*BOOM!*" *Oh God, don't panic*, Kate commanded her mind. "Tobias, did that man give this to you?"

The frightened child cringed with a whimper, as his other hand went to his swollen shirt.

Kate's fingers slid to the chest of the child and felt a hard box. She ripped open his vest and shirt with such ferocity that the buttons popped off. She found a well-crafted bomb made of the mysterious green liquid, wires, cogs, and a moving pocket watch that was twined to his body. The time was poised at exactly one minute to noon.

Kate took a knife from her pocket and struggled with the thick layers of prickly twine as she spoke to the petrified child. "Tobias, when I get this off you, run as far as you can. Go back home to Sister Teresa."

"No, Miss Kate, I can't." His eyes were wide with fear. Kate was halfway through the mess when the second hand on the clock face was moving faster than she liked. She was positive that they'd set it to go off at noon.

"Okay then, just go anywhere, okay? Just run, as fast as you can!" And with that, the twine rope snapped, and she ripped the explosive off. "Run!" she screamed and took off to the pump behind the saloon. She tossed the bomb into the horse trough next to the water pump and jumped into the back of the saloon. Kate took cover under a table and waited as her heart pounded through her chest. She heard the wires pop and hiss as the chilly water consumed the device, effectively stopping it.

Kate crawled out and listened. She heard town folk and horses in the street, but no further sounds from Drasco's gang. They were focused on the letters and cash they'd received and hadn't seen Drasco at the other end of the drag.

He could've killed more people.

She slid alongside the building, peered round the corner, and was relieved at the events unfolding.

They were whispering and smiling, hurrying back home to pack. Kate ran back to the bomb, gathered it from the trough, dried it, and took it to her room. She had an idea, but she had tasks to finish before Drasco came back. As Kate left, she felt that something-is-horribly wrong feeling, in the pit of her stomach. *Where did Tobias run to?*

She briefly checked to see that the streets completely cleared out. On a hunch, Kate crossed to the backside of one of the empty buildings. She was stealthy with a pistol in hand as she approached the near-empty orphanage next door. She tapped to no avail. Kate's hands twitched at her gun holsters. *What happened to Sister Teresa?*

She tried the door, paused, and entered the building. It was deathly quiet. "Sister? Sister Teresa?" Kate called. No answer. She spied into the parlor and kitchen, both empty. Perhaps they left? But her heart told her otherwise. She headed upstairs to the sleeping quarters. In each room, the beds were neatly made save one, most likely Tobias's.

Kate approached the bedroom at the end of the hall and found remnants of what she'd feared. Sister Theresa's room was violently disturbed. A broken lamp and her Bible were discarded recklessly on the floor. Her bed had been stripped, the covers missing. "Oh no." Kate moaned and slid to the floor. She let herself break down, the tears coming easily. *No wonder Tobias refused to come back. What had he seen?*

After a few moments, Kate collected herself, scooped up the sister's Bible, and crept out of the home unseen. She must not be emotional, she reminded herself. She realized saving the whole town was impossible and it was obviously too late here. God knows what they did with the saintly woman.

Kate headed to the saloon. A drink might calm her.

Yep, I need a dose of spirits, she decided.

Ellie stumbled down the interior saloon stairs and into the bar, obviously hung over. The sassy Southern bar owner was still in her nightdress in midafternoon but did not care in the least. "Well, hello Miss Iris Gambler." Ellie slurred pleasantly.

"Um, looks like the lady's been dipping into her own till." Kate laughed.

"And you look like shit," Ellie teased. "Damn it, Kate, I swear, do you have to wrestle these guys too? Isn't poker enough? You even dress like a dude now." She noticed her friend's rumpled appearance and cuts and bruises appeared from underneath the cosmetics. Her brown eyes grew softer as Kate remained silent. "I'm sorry Kate," she intoned politely. "I've had enough. I'm leaving. I sent my last two girls out yesterday."

Kate grimaced and shook her head.

"Please tell me you're leaving?" Ellie pleaded.

"Yep, I came in for one last drink." Kate laughed.

Ellie returned her mirth. "Okay, what'll you'll have? Uh…wait, what do I have left?" The bar mistress laughed. "Oh, I have a bottle of absinthe. It'll knock you on your ass. Well, I know you've probably already been on it, but here—it'll make your ass feel better." Ellie poured two shots. The women toasted "to Iris" and downed the sweet liquor. Several shots were downed until they'd emptied the bottle. "Alright then, I have to pack. See you at the train?"

"Yep, be careful Ellie." Kate hugged her friend.

"You too missy!" Ellie waved the lady maverick out.

Whoa, that was delicious, Kate was mirthful in mind.

Unfortunately for Ellie, Kate in an inebriated state, crawled upstairs in the afternoon sun, and collapsed into a restful nap. She did not hear a member of Drasco's gang cover the saloon owner's mouth with a poisoned cloth moments later. The deranged cowpoke dragged Ellie's dying body to a storage room under the staircase, where he had his way with her and branded her like the others. He left the saloon owner's broken body in that room, finally getting what he wanted. Drasco promised the miscreant that he'd have the saloon owner when he joined the gang. His tawdry and sick opportunity had risen as the town emptied. Once he finished his evil deeds, the filthy, twisted cowpoke whooped maniacally as he rode off to meet his cohorts.

Kate awoke for the second time that day as the sun hung low in the sky. She stood up hastily and tripped to the washstand. It was 4:30 p.m. She tidied up, chewed on jerky, and once again watched from the window.

She then left the room to get fresh air and feed Sonny. She heard the bustle of persons heading for the post. The roar of the train sounded its arrival.

Amen. Kate smiled with relief as she walked to the edge of the saloon. She did what had become routine—surveyed the area and felt a pair of eyes on her. The undertaker stopped in her direction on his way to the train.

Kate nodded a welcome.

"Well, Miss Church, I only had one body left to bury."

The tilt of her head and a confused look caused the undertaker to continue.

"The Johnsons were leaving their ranch and stopped for water at the creek before leaving town via wagon. They found that Negro boy hung in a tree not far from where the Chinese couple lived." He paused, seeing Kate's face flush.

She bit her lip from the inside to hide her rising vitriol. Speak, she contained herself. Slowly the words came to her. "It was Tobias?"

He watched her eyes become steady blue pools.

"Yes. They cut him down and brought him to me about an hour ago. I had just enough time to put him near the church. I'm sorry." He was genuine and his voice changed to a whisper. He wiped his withered forehead and bald head with a kerchief and put on his best top hat.

"Thank you," Kate replied stoically. "Have a safe trip, sir."

He turned to leave, but then stopped to look at the woman who had made many sacrifices.

"You gotta quit doing my job for me, Miss Church. You can't keep putting these men in the ground. Even I know my work is done here." He touched her shoulder with a cold hand. It was like death was reaching out to her, telling her to leave.

"I know. Thank you." Kate was embraced in the gold of the setting sun. Her curls blew loosely around her shoulders in an approaching sunset wind. She appeared angelic and rested. Kate wasn't afraid. She'd fulfilled her promise to Riley. "Goodbye, sir."

"Goodbye, Miss Church. Godspeed." As the undertaker ambled towards the train, Kate watched the sunset.

I may cry, she promised herself, *but they will never own me.* Chin's voice echoed in her head "You strong now" as darkness fell upon Iris.

13 A KIDNAPPING AND AN OFFER

Kate was spent. Her mind reeled from the past day's events as she flopped down on the bed, exhausted. She pressed her fingertips to her temples in an attempt to stop the pounding in her head. The ache in her body ran from head to toe. It hurt to even pull off her boots.

The violence had been horrid. Who in God's name killed children? Oh, it was Drasco, but no way to prove it and no proper way to bring him to justice.

She was assured that he was aware of the benefactor if he had killed Tobias. He may have seen Tobias giving her the invitations. And in turn, he'd ambushed her with a fake. Now Strax was dead, her beloved canine poisoned. He'd done the same to Ming and Chin. What savage evil had been unleashed on Iris. It scorched her heart and soul.

Kate cried out in angst as her emotions caught up with her. Her body shook with sobs. When she finished, she remembered Chin's advice to breathe. She inhaled and let the crisp evening air fill her lungs. She stood and wiped down at the washstand.

It was time to escape. The remaining residents of Iris received their notes and cash. She surmised they'd carry on. Ferris left to marry Abby. It'd be a blessing if they were wed before her father passed. *He should be halfway to St. Louis by now.*

Kate held just enough cash to get back home, pay off the remainder of her family's debts, and start over. She spent the evening preparing her weapons, packing, and pulling out that black dress she saved for special occasions. She'd exit tomorrow, leaving word for the benefactor at the post.

Just as she closed her eyes to rest, creaking floorboards outside the door startled her. Kate froze, not moving an inch. The whisper of paper and footsteps leaving down the stairs caught her attention. An invitation has been tucked under her door. She waited a moment, her head cocked sideways straining to hear of any further commotion. She then picked up the familiar crisp parchment and seal. She read:

"*Dear Miss Church,*

In light of current events, I have an urgent task for you. I have a contact who will meet with you at midnight tonight at the dock of the creek by the church. He will have instructions for you then; prepare for a long evening. Come alone, but armed. If this reaches you beyond midnight tonight, I will have other instructions for you at the Post tomorrow. Perhaps you will be ready to complete a task this evening?

Sincerely,

W."

Her heart thumped wildly. It was already 11:15 p.m. She packed in the dark, including her satchel, a flask, a blanket, a lamp, her pistol, and whip. She changed into her standard rail wear to avoid suspicion. Drasco and his men could be anywhere. She slid out of the room and down the outside to Sonny. Her horse peeked up expectantly when she untied the lead. She mounted and rode only in the moonlight until she was at the church. She tied Sonny and lit her lamp. With a tight grip on her whip handle, Kate scanned around the area and took the short path down to the creek bed.

Several trees lined that path and Kate prepared for a possible ambush. Just as that concern crossed her mind, everything went black as a sack was tossed over her head. She began to scream, but a hand covered her mouth.

"Shhh, listen, I won't hurt you." a lilting male voice whispered, "Can you hear me?"

"Mmmm." Kate bobbed her head and listened to the masculine voice.

"I am your contact from your benefactor, I promise I am not here to do you harm. Please keep your voice down. Do you understand, you must trust me?"

She nodded and the contact lifted his hand from her mouth.

"You must leave the sack on, but I will lead you. We can't stay here, but I can't tell you where we're going." The contact had a warm British accent and a firm hand, which led her back up the path to a flatbed. She hadn't seen it behind the church when she'd arrived. He put out her lamp and loaded it and the satchel into the wagon. "I'm lifting you into the back. Just lie down and relax. Please be cooperative and leave the sack on."

Kate whispered a quiet "Yes" and the contact picked her up and placed her inside. She felt the warmth of a blanket as he covered her from the cool night desert air. She heard him close the tailgate and pull himself atop. He made a "click, click" noise and the horse cantered off at a brisk pace. The sack formed a screen over her eyes, and she nearly made out the full harvest moon and bright stars.

Kate had no idea of the time or where they were headed, but she gathered it was safe. She realized she had easily given herself over to a total stranger but was oddly at ease. The rocking of the ride relaxed Kate and she began to drift off to sleep when it stopped. Kate heard the contact tether the horse.

His dusty tracks crunched round the back. He slid the gate down. "Alright then, Miss Church, sit up for a moment please." He spoke in a tender British accent. She did as asked and felt his firm hands pull her to him. He seemed to lift her easily. *He must be strong.*

Her heart fluttered in excitement. He set the lamp down. Light filtered through the sack that smelled of corn. "Here now," he intoned, "I will lead you in." He guided her forward, "Now, up and wait." He held her steady. Kate heard the jangle of keys and the creak of a wooden door. "Okay, inside now," and he gripped her hand and led her. "Just a few and we'll sit you down then." She heard the door close behind her.

"Now, just a moment." He helped her to a wooden chair.

She managed to see his silhouette when he set the lamp down and approached her.

"I'm taking the sack off. Close your eyes a moment. Then your eyes can adjust, yes please?"

"Yes," she replied as goose bumps tickled her skin. *He could kill me, leave me here, dead for days and no one would ever know.*

He whipped off the sack with a flourish and her hat with it. He scooped up the boater and placed it on the table. And then, for the first time, the contact got a solid look at her up close. Her curly blonde locks fell haphazardly from her hat and draped long over her shoulders. Her eyes blinked, she rubbed them, and they popped open, bright blue. She wore trousers, black boots, long brown gloves, and a white blouse covered with a long tan leather coat which made her appear smaller in person. Kate was armed indeed, a pistol and whip at her hip. And she was beautiful. She appeared younger than her supposed thirty-six years. Her skin glowed in the lamplight. The contact felt like he had just woken a cherub from a heavenly nap. With a smattering of cuts and bruises visible, it appeared she recovered well from the incident with Drasco, *that nasty bastard.*

"Miss Church, I apologize for all of the secrecy. I am Mr. Bartlett, your contact to your benefactor, who we'll call Mr. W for now. Can I offer you water or perhaps a brandy?"

Kate peered at the contact as he evolved from the dark room. He was tall, with brown hair with a neat goatee, a mustache, and piercing blue-green eyes. He wore a brown suit and vest. She recognized him as he brought a chair forward.

"You were at the saloon?" Kate stuttered, "You were...are, Mr. King?"

"Yes, I am. You are quite observant, Miss Church." He registered his cohort's appearance and continued, "Mr. W heard of your astute qualities and asked that I meet you. A drink, then?"

"Yes please, water," she was stunned that someone had desired her so much that they were willing to travel so far.

He brought out a kettle and two cups from a dark corner of the room. He poured still warm water for them both.

"Well Miss Church, let us have a brief discussion then." And so it began, the first of many Discussions betwixt the two. He drank then spoke, "Your discretion is of the utmost importance.

Should you see me after this meeting, in town or anywhere near it, you should still refer to me as Mr. King, is that understood?" he directed in such a severe fashion that she awoke to the seriousness of the situation at hand.

"Yes." Kate shifted uneasily.

"Your benefactor has been pleased with your actions and how you've performed your duties. However, the town has become increasingly hazardous. You've realized the danger of this Mr. Drasco fellow and his gang?"

"Yes, I have." Kate was briskly reminded of the pain Drasco caused. Just the reminder of him made her jaw lock.

"We have a reliable belief that you are no longer safe here. Am I correct? You've most likely lost several friends, acquaintances, and the like?"

"I think you know this already…" she responded warily. There was no doubt that Mr. Bartlett had been watching her since she was first contacted. Unbeknownst to Kate, Mr. Bartlett was the gentleman that had come a great distance for her. "If I should stay, I may not live much longer," Kate filled with tension. Her fingers grazed instinctively over her holster with the threat of danger.

"I have made your benefactor, Mr. W, aware of this. He is well impressed with your skills and wishes to hire you in a similar capacity for an extended period. He is in the condition to help you leave town. He has asked that I extend you an offer, one that I, unfortunately, cannot convey to you on paper as his discretion is of the highest value. He has two tasks to be handled immediately and then if all is well and completed as expected, he may have a permanent position for you." Kate listened intently and leaned forward in her chair. "I am certain you have questions, but first I must tell you, I may not answer them. Mr. W. values your trust in him and entreats that you'd consider such an offer."

"How, when, and what amount should I expect? Please pardon my inquiry, but I must weigh my options." The words tumbled from her mouth. *Am I really in this dark cabin in the cool desert in the middle of the night?*

"Miss Church, the offer is high, $10,000 for each. But by participating in them you will put yourself in grave conditions. You must be willing to follow any instructions exactly. Indecision kills." He was stern and serious, his lips pursed. "You must leave on the five-p.m. train tomorrow. Should you accept this offer, a package containing a ticket, instructions and enough travel expenses will be waiting for you at the post. Pick it up by three p.m. You must be on the train; you will be heading back East. The destination will be revealed in the package. Dress like a lady to the post, disguise yourself and tell no one that you are leaving. Leave your horse tethered behind the building. Once you leave the post, do not under any circumstances turn back. Will you consider this offer?" He saw that Kate was overwhelmed, with exhaustion in her eyes, but it was clear that her time was limited.

Mr. Bartlett needed to extract her before Drasco took action. She possessed abilities that Mr. W. desired. Physically she'd dealt with heat, impossible personalities, horrific violence, and yet remained hearty and feminine. Emotionally she was stalwart, but she had a genteel heart—a perfect balance for the tasks at hand. She was not too hard; she was not too soft. He hoped she'd accept.

"I will," she was firm.

"I like your confidence, Miss Church, but you can render your decision by catching the train tomorrow, is that understood?"

He worried about her slipping away or, heaven forbid, getting killed.

"Yes, yes I do," Kate responded clearly, realizing only fools turned down $20,000. She could go home to St. Louis afterward, join Abby and Ferris, and live comfortably.

"Well then, I must bring you back. Thank you for your consideration, Miss Church." He took her hand, pulled back her glove, and kissed it.

She was taken aback by the wet warmth of his lips tickling her skin. He was a real English gentleman. *Mr. W. must be spectacular as well.*

"For your safety, allow me to cover you again please? You know if you are ever questioned, you cannot lie about where you've been. There are those who recognize liars in an instant and I don't want to put you in that position."

"Yes, of course," Kate replied, and the sack was returned over her head. He lowered the lamp, led her out in the cool night to the wagon, and placed her in. She reclined and was amazed at how quickly her life was changing.

Mr. Bartlett started the horses and grinned under the stars. She was obedient, she was pretty—she was perfect.

They arrived at the church, and he helped her to Sonny. The horse whinnied as they approached.

Mr. Bartlett held her shoulders from behind. "Now Miss Church, I'm lifting the sack," he whispered. "You are to leave directly and not look back, is that understood?"

"Yes, thank you." She stood firmly and listened.

"Very well. I will see you soon Miss Church. Take care and Godspeed." He helped her mount as her eyes adjusted to the moon, still bright in the sky. She rode into the dark and focused forward as ordered. Mr. Bartlett sighed, grateful that she complied. He whispered to himself, "Don't be too soft, Miss Kate." He was positive that they hadn't been watched this time. Drasco had caught on to his invitations and it cost lives. He'd had to act now. Their clandestine meeting went as planned.

He exhaled deeply as the wagon bumped along in the desert away in the opposite direction. He was enthralled with the prospect of employing Miss Church.

14 EXODUS

The day of the rail office closing dawned pleasantly. The rising autumn sun poured through the window with a wind leisurely blowing the curtains. Kate was exhausted, having had no sleep the night before. After she visited with Mr. Bartlett, she shuffled her belongings to Ellie's room above the saloon. Her limbs ached to the point where lifting her satchel and trunk took extra effort.

But she didn't sleep in Ellie's bed; Kate pushed it in front of the door, should Drasco's gang mount an early morning attack. She put on Ferris's suit to sleep in and used her jacket as a blanket, resting fitfully on the floor. As the sun rose, she took out her writing ink, about half a bottle, and dyed her hair in Ellie's washbasin. Her once golden locks were coal black. She painted her skin, covering any bit of physical damage done by Drasco and his gang. With delicate strokes of Kate's fingers, a pleasant face appeared in the mirror.

Kate dressed like a lady, as her benefactor requested. The black satin dress with a bustle and train that she saved was serving its purpose today. Combined with an exquisite hat topped with a satin bow and thick veils, and a heavier parasol with a rather unique handle, Kate had her perfect disguise, one she long ago prepared for her advantage. The smooth black fabric felt intoxicating on her skin. She straightened as the lace on the high collar that teased her jawline. She picked up an elegant bag that a saloon girl had left behind. The handles were sturdy to the touch and easily held the weight of her curious items. It now contained the necessary tools for her journey.

She used extreme caution in descending the main stairs of the saloon, each step executed with genteel purpose. *Thank God Ellie left.*

Unbeknownst to her, Ellie's deceased body drew insects and vermin beneath the very stairs she strolled down.

After feeding her beloved equine, Kate untethered Sonny and led him behind the main buildings to the post. The leather reins were wrapped loosely around her gloves and her heart ached knowing that this was the final moment with her beloved steed. By nine a.m. she promptly strode inside the post, nodding to its nervous owner, who tapped his feet impatiently. He was both politely astounded that she'd come early and at Kate's lovely appearance. He didn't recognize her from the day before.

She lifted the dark veils and winked at her contact.

This time there wasn't much left to be said. The postman handed her the package from Mr. Bartlett and she, in turn, handed him a bag of apples. He raised an eyebrow.

Kate waved at the steed. "The horse's name is Sonny."

He tipped his hat, and as Kate left the post, he locked the door behind her. He gathered the remaining envelopes from Kate addressed to Sister Theresa and Ellie, pocketed the funds, and rolled the letters and envelopes to assist in lighting his pipe. He had been informed by the gentleman that unfortunately neither lady was coming in for a ticket. He enjoyed a smoke at the back of the post before stomping out the ashes, hanging up his apron, and grabbing a specially packed satchel. He came out from behind the building, greeted his ride out of town, "Hello Sonny," and proffered a sweet apple to the beast. After the final bite, the postman peered round with piercing eyes, mounted, and left Iris unseen.

Kate sashayed across the street, having turned down the long veils of the hat to protect her newly powdered skin from the rising sun. She made a brief stop before her last destination in Iris, Drasco's warehouse full of the green volatile liquids. Kate was in and out, completely unseen, and headed for the orphans' home. As she expected, no one found her. She sat on a chaise while waiting in the darkened parlor and let her fingers thump and stroke the velvety fabric. She'd drawn the heavy curtains with a slit to peer out. Occasionally, she squinted at the empty street and then exhaled, relieved that Iris was silent.

Within a couple of hours, Drasco's gang roared into town and vanquished the liquor and cigars they'd raided from Ellie's packed steamer trunk. When the noontime train arrived, they made their way to the station. Only a rancher and the owners of the hotel departed from the platform. "Where is she?" Drasco hissed under his breath. "That bitch. Check around boys," his voice grew louder as the train rolled away. The gang split off, spreading as far out as the church and creek to find Kate, but to no avail.

"Her horse is gone," complained the corrupt cowboy that killed Ellie.

"Nah, she let it run off," Drasco wondered aloud. "C'mon, let's get grub." They retreated to the saloon to wait, drinking and playing poker until the noise of the five-p.m. train startled them.

The remaining handful hurried to the station. Less than seven people including the widow prepared to board. A rising tension filled the air as Drasco, and his gang approached the platform. The conductor returned to collect tickets, watching the bandits out of the corner of his eye. He was dodging trouble on this stop. He had an important passenger to collect.

"Everyone's leaving, eh?" Drasco mused aloud.

Filled with fear, no one dared to respond.

"Well, that's fine," he mocked to his crew under his breath, "I don't need anyone else digging in my business like that bitch. She must be here," he reasoned. "She didn't leave with anyone else. She was too stupid to protect herself."

As the widow passed her ticket to the coachman, Drasco piped up, "Even the widow is leaving. No more funerals, eh widow?" The woman in black stopped for a moment but did not look directly at her aggressor.

"No sir," she politely replied, swiftly boarding the train.

A bawling child distracted the paltry group as a family of three arrived just in time.

"Sorry, mister," the family's father apologized to the conductor. "Colic with the baby, but he's alright now." And indeed, the child stopped crying.

"No problem, sir, please watch your step." The conductor held the expected number of tickets. "All aboard!" he shouted for the last time in Iris.

Drasco was dumbfounded. He and his gang watched the train roll out of the station as the sun set. "Shit," he mumbled under his breath, "I want every nook and cranny of this town checked."

But before Drasco and his motley crew of cowboys could move, seconds later, at precisely 5:05 p.m. an immense explosion from the precariously filled warehouse rocked the town like an earthquake. A massive orange fireball engulfed the building across from the saloon effectively blowing it to bits. Its glow reflected on the rattled windows of the safely departed train.

Passengers gasped and craned their necks to see the resulting destruction. All were jolted but one. Beneath the thick veils of the widow's elegant hat, Kate Church smiled.

Kate had never liked funerals, but when the town changed, she covertly began using that black dress for special occasions. Those times happened to be the days when select residents left Iris in a less than pleasant fashion to the greater beyond. Kate was only sad she hadn't worn it at Riley's passing. It would have destroyed her only way of knowing what was truly happening in Iris. And mourners loved to chat at funerals, the perfect opportunity to eavesdrop in plain sight. It was funny how no one ever questioned her while dressed as the widow. Death had an odd way of bringing the town together and opening their mouths about the newly departed.

Fireballs erupted in the encroaching dusk as the train churned on. The former residents stared out their windows until the devastation was behind them. They then turned their attention to their future. They still hadn't a clue that their emancipator sat among them.

Kate planned her escape well. She couldn't kill Drasco, but she could make his life in Iris difficult after she'd left. His whole inventory of collected explosives was obliterated, effectively disappointing his partners in crime.

When Kate crept inside the warehouse after leaving the post, she'd placed a plain package amongst the tube-filled seed bags resting on a long bench under the front window. In the serenity of the dangerously quiet room, if one had listened closely, they might've heard a steady ticking. She retrieved the bomb meant to kill her, fixed its mechanisms, and effectively used it on Drasco and his gang.

As the passengers settled into seats after witnessing the destruction of the town they once loved, the conductor efficiently checked the tickets in his stack. The ticket on top was marked with a simple "W" on the back. He strode down the aisle, offering candy to the children and upon passing Kate, gave the slightest nod.

Kate adjusted her hat in return and the conductor moved on. "Boom indeed," she whispered to herself.

15 NACOGDOCHES

The steady rhythm of the train lulled Kate into the best sleep she'd had in years. The rail car was still, especially after a hearty dinner of roast chicken, potatoes, and greens that had been served to its occupants. Wine and spirits were poured liberally. How wonderful that the lowliest of Iris were feasting like royalty. After the passengers had fallen into blissful slumber near midnight, the conductor surveyed the car and then tapped the shoulder of his charge. He was a tall, lean young man, with an angular jawline, freckles, copper hair, and a short mustache.

Kate jolted awake, her grip taut on her parasol handle. The conductor put a finger to his lips. She lifted her veils to see better in the dimly lit locomotive. The conductor was pleasantly astonished at her beauty; his contact had been correct in describing his special guest. He motioned for Kate to come forward and took her bag. He made a comical face at its heavy weight. She carried her parasol under her arm and strode behind him.

The conductor led her to a private seating area in the car ahead and followed her in whilst closing the door. Two plush plum-colored upholstered chairs, a round wooden table with brass trim, and a storage drawer lined the room. Velvet dark green tasseled curtains framed the window. He drew them and waved her to sit, "Are you comfortable Miss Church?"

"Yes, thank you." She set her parasol upright next to her chair.

His face became a mask of seriousness.

"You are to read what's in your package now. If you have any questions about your invitation, let me know. May I check your bag?" Assuming he would simply place her items in a storage compartment, Kate agreed.

Instead, the conductor opened her bag as Kate's mouth fell open. He twittered. "You needn't fret. Just checking that you have enough accessories for your trip. I am not here to judge." He dumped out makeup, two Bibles, a silken nightgown, a sheathed knife, a rather unique pistol, a whip, the package from Mr. Bartlett, apples, and jerky. The variety of expressions as he pulled out her collection of items was entertaining. "I see that you are well prepared." He was amused that such a pleasant woman had such an interesting cache of weaponry, and yet two Bibles. "Tea, madam?"

"Yes please," she responded happily; it was nice to be served.

His tone returned to concern.

"When I come back, listen for two short, then three long knocks announcing my return. Should there be any other combination during this trip, you should prepare for the worst. If we should cross other passengers on this voyage, simply refer to me as Porter. Now I'll leave you to read your invitations in private."

Kate opened the package that had been tucked in her bag. It contained the standard letter marked "Read at once" with the usual wax seal, plenty of cash, and two other smaller letters with "Engagement #1" and "Engagement #2" written on them in W.'s familiar script. She read the letter first as requested.

"Dear Miss Church:

I trust that you are well in your travels today. Thank you for your continued service. Enclosed you will find two Engagements. You are not to open the second Engagement until you have safely completed the first. Open any documents only in a secured secluded area.

Each one should be handled with the utmost care and discretion. Any deviance from the enclosed assignments will cost a reduction in pay and most importantly, your life. Please take heed in continuing to follow the standard previous rules. Rest and eat properly when time allows. A weak person cannot complete strong work.

Do not share details with any of your other contacts during these Engagements. They are for tactical support only.

You may read your first Engagement now.

Best of luck on your journey, Miss Church. Be safe.

Sincerely,

W."

With trembling hands, Kate folded the letter and opened the first Engagement. She was interrupted by a series of knocks, two short, three long. It was Porter; she relaxed. Kate set the package and papers in her lap as he came in with a cup of tea, a pitcher, cream, and sugar, all in fine china on an ornate wooden and brass tray. "Here you are, Miss Church, enjoy. I will be back in the morning to collect your tray and bring in breakfast at nine a.m. The neighboring compartment has a bed and water closet, but if you could bear it, it would be wise of you to sleep here in case any of the other passengers should wander."

"This will do," she replied kindly. She sank into the comfortable furnishing. The bed she'd slept in for twenty years made her appreciate the chair's plush cushioning.

"Well then, a quilt is in the drawer. Have a pleasant evening ma'am." The conductor left, closing the door nary a sound.

Kate poured her tea, adding cream and sugar, then finished her reading as she sipped the deliciously warm drink. The first Engagement included a short instructional letter, a blank card, a pen, ink, and a picture of what appeared to be a Spanish-inspired church.

She read the letter:

"Engagement #1

Miss Church, you are to take the train to Nacogdoches, Texas. It should arrive late morning tomorrow. Be dressed as if mourning and well-disguised. You have this costume prepared already. Act like a lady at all times.

A driver will meet you at the station. He will have a black horse and a simple brown carriage. You will know him by the bluebonnets tucked into his coachman's hat. You'll nod to him and adjust your hat. He will drive you to your destination which should be an approximately forty-five-minute ride.

You will arrive at a Mission just North of Nacogdoches. Approach quietly and go to the convent to the far right of the church. A picture of the church is enclosed in this Engagement. There will be a statue of Mary, the Mother of Our Lord in front. Knock only three times and wait. Sister Rosa will be waiting for your arrival. She will speak to you but not address you by name and will lead you to the body of Sister Theresa. Once alone with the body, you are to briefly confirm that it is her and see if she was marked with Drasco's brand. This should only extend to five minutes; any longer will cause undue suspicion. When you are done, return immediately to your driver. Do not pause, and do not look back.

On your return trip in the carriage, briefly note on the enclosed card as to what you have seen, "yes" that it was her and if the brand is there, "no" if not. Tuck this in your bag. You will give it to the same conductor, at the same station, but for a new train that will depart for Kansas City at 3 p.m. the same day.

Of the utmost importance: should your conductor or driver be displaced or not attend; you will be at the mercy of your own cleverness. I have enclosed emergency funds. Only in this case should you open Engagement #2 so as not to miss your next connection.

Sincerely,

W."

Kate caught her breath. It was obvious that Mr. Bartlett had watched her enough to know that she was the widow. She sighed heavily; she didn't like being observed. Hmm, this might be hard, she pondered, except for the dark clothes of course. But any harder than dealing with death on a daily basis and running from a ruthless gang?

She studied the photo for a moment, cementing the details in her mind, and stashed the packet back into her bag. Kate removed her hat and placed it on the neighboring chair with a knowing smile. She deftly loosened her corset with a whoosh of breath. She let her hands embrace the embroidered beauty of her quilt. Her nimble fingers tidied her hair and covered herself. Within moments she was fast asleep.

Promptly at nine a.m. Porter rapped in proper order to the private compartment discreetly hiding Kate from the other passengers. Kate woke, sat up, and adjusted herself in the chair as the conductor brought a breakfast of eggs, ham, toast, and fresh tea. "Good morning, Miss Church. The other passengers are being served breakfast also, now might be a splendid time to tidy up." He tilted his head towards the neighboring compartment.

"Yes, thank you." She stood as Porter double-checked the narrow passage. He held the door and waved a hand towards the water closet. Kate speedily checked herself at the closet's tiny washstand. With nimble flicks of her fingers, she deemed herself presentable. She was famished and ready to eat. The conductor led her back and briefly, instructed her on the day's activities. He threw open the curtains to a sunny autumn day. "You have an hour to eat, after which the train will arrive in Nacogdoches. I will knock when you can safely depart and complete your Engagement."

"Thank you." Kate hungrily devoured her meal as he left. The flavors melted deliciously in her mouth as she reread the Engagement instructions. She then readied her bag, smoothed her dress with delicate hands, put on her hat with zest, and watched the world zip by in the window as the train sped along. The land gave way to ranches and towns, then groups of larger buildings. The train slowed and the hiss of the steam engine ceased.

Kate heard the excited chatter of her former neighbors departing. *God bless them,* she intoned. Moments later, the conductor's precise rap came abruptly. He opened the door without a word as Kate stood ready to leave, pulling down the veils of her hat. He pointed to the nearest exit and tipped his cap.

Kate stepped out into the mid-morning sun. It briefly reminded her of her arrival in Iris. She watched the platform's activity. Most of the train's other passengers were well on their way to their future destinations. Off to her right, she found her driver, wearing a black cap with attached fresh bluebonnets. She adjusted her hat with a nod and hopped into her waiting carriage. It was simple indeed, brown with standard wheels, a leather bench seat, and an adjustable accordion cover which was placed in the down position.

"Good afternoon, ma'am. Please allow me." Her driver proffered a stool, dispensed her into the vehicle, and drew up the cover. His passenger should not be seen.

"Thank you, sir," Kate responded. She appeared relaxed. She was prepared to begin this engagement.

"We're off then." And the carriage was on its way. The ride to the Mission was uneventful and Kate paused to reflect. Her situation was precarious, she contemplated. *What am I doing here?* All she'd known, her friends, and family were far away or dead. This was a means to a better end, she reassured herself. It was time to focus.

In the distance, the Mission bell rang at eleven a.m. They were right on time. The Mission stood in a city of buildings surrounded by a white wall protecting its inhabitants. The iron gate was open, and the driver drove the carriage through to a plaza of red brick and well-kept gardens. It was quiet except for a stone fountain trickling fresh spring water and chirping birds that were enjoying the warm sunshine. Her driver dismounted from his perch and wordlessly offered his hand. She acknowledged him with a nod and entered the Mission grounds. As promised, the church, the convent, and the Mary statue stood out in the heat. Kate strode purposefully to the nuns' quarters and knocked three times as ordered.

It was quiet enough that she heard the approaching footsteps of her contact from outside a heavy wooden plank door. Sister Rosa answered as expected. "Good morning, welcome to the Mission." She was dressed in a pure white habit which highlighted her Spanish tan skin. Sister Rosa was an older woman, possibly in her fifties, with pleasant wrinkles and a serene smile.

"Good morning, Sister," Kate replied evenly.

"This way," her contact guided her into the convent. It was made of the same white walls and brick as the exterior. The main hall was lined with religious art, mosaics, and windows that let sunshine reflect on the beauty of the building's inside. Sister Rosa led Kate down the full length of the hall to an open narrow doorway and a spiral staircase.

The ladies walked briskly down the stairs into a cellar hallway lined with several doors. Sister Rosa lit a lamp waiting for them on a table at the bottom. "We have storage here," Sister Rosa explained. "Our order does many charitable deeds." They walked the full length of the building to a dark heavy wooden door at the end. The nun unhitched a set of keys from her belt and unlocked it. "You'll find what you need in here. I will wait outside." She paused, opened the door, ushered Kate in, and then closed it behind her. The cellar room was surprisingly bright from a high window that was just above the ground level outside. It was cool inside.

Kate sighed as she approached the body covered in a crisp white sheet on a long wooden table in the direct center of the room. *Oh no.* The sudden realization of what she must do cut in her gut. She exhaled, steadied herself, crossed to the sister, and briskly tugged down the sheet at the head. Instantly she knew, it was indeed Sister Teresa, dressed in full habit. Kate saw a wooden rosary tucked in the deceased sister's gloved hands. The holy woman beheld a simplistic beauty. Her facial skin was still flawless, and her eyes closed as if sleeping.

Kate recovered the head, turned to the foot of the table, and lifted the sheet with care. Sister Theresa's narrow feet peeked out from under her long white skirt. Kate dreaded what she was charged to do next, her body taut with anticipation. *Breathe,* she lifted the garment. Kate choked back tears as she revealed scrapes and bruises over both legs of the departed sister. She gathered the clothing up further, lifted the stiff body ever so, and peeked under the right buttock cheek.

The mark of the devil on earth. Drasco had branded her.

What else had they done to her? Oh, evil bastard, Kate felt her ire ascending furiously. She grit her teeth as her eyes blurred with tears.

Respectfully, Kate readjusted Sister Theresa's gown and her funeral drape. For a moment she clutched the edge of the table in such a harsh manner that her fingertips burned. "Dear God, I don't understand this madness," she prayed, "but I hope that you have given this faithful servant the eternal peace she deserves. Amen." Kate bowed and whispered through the cloth, "Goodbye dear Sister." She turned and opened the door to Sister Rosa with a pained expression.

"It is done," Kate spoke tersely. The nun led her guest back upstairs and to the entrance of the convent. Under the veils, Kate's blood boiled. Sister Rosa, sensing Kate's rage, hesitated for a moment before opening the door and ruffled Kate by lifting her veils. Kate bit her lip but refused to hide her displeasure at finding another violent death at the hands of Drasco.

Sister Rosa looked directly into Kate's revealed eyes. "Justice is mine sayeth the Lord." Then kindly, "Please take care. God bless you, child." She opened the door.

Kate tugged her veils down and spoke stiffly. "Sister, you are far more forgiving than I. God bless you and the Mission. Thank you and good day." Kate walked out briskly to the carriage.

Sister Rosa muttered under her breath as the departing contact approached her ride, "Don't be too hard, Miss Church."

They'll like her, the holy woman mused, but the new Member had to learn to control her anger.

The driver jumped down; they were on schedule, but storm clouds loomed in the distance. He hustled to prevent getting caught in a deluge. She gave the customary nod, and within minutes the carriage was on its way back to Nacogdoches. The sun was in a halo of cirrus clouds as Kate noted her card for Mr. Bartlett:

"Yes, on both accounts."

A perfect answer—no names, no outstanding details should the card fall into the wrong hands. Kate tucked the card and her writing accessories into her bag. Her veils swayed in the breeze as the winds picked up. The sky darkened with frightening rapidity and the rumble of thunder rolled in the distance.

"It appears as if we're in for a hard rain, ma'am." The driver's brow wrinkled with anxiety as he alerted Kate.

"Carry on, please, if we can," Kate spoke firmly. They couldn't go back to the Mission, and they were now in an area of sparsely populated ranches. The driver slapped his horse with a crop and the carriage began to pick up the pace. The sky was now an ugly green grey and a particularly fierce gale swayed the wagon. It began to rain—plump drops that splattered angrily into the dirt and plopped on the carriage cover. Suddenly the heavens opened, raining sheets and hail, pelting the driver and carriage. The cover was wholly inappropriate for the inclement weather and Kate was getting soaked.

The horse was becoming testy, slowing to a trot. "Ma'am, we must seek cover immediately!" the driver shouted over the roaring weather.

"Yes, anywhere!" she called in return. Searching through the nasty downpour, she saw a barn on the left side of the road. "There!"

The driver caught sight of it and turned into a side path with no gravel, only dirt which was rapidly thickening to mud. The steed whinnied in protest, but the driver managed to pull up to the barn. Surprising her guide, Kate sprang from the carriage and ran to the barn door. Speedily she unbolted the lock with a firm jolt. The driver hastily drove the carriage in, jumped down, and tethered the horse. Kate shut the door just as the wind became violent.

She examined their shelter, her eyes checking for possible occupancy. It became obvious that the barn hadn't been used for some time. A couple of brittle hay bales were disintegrating to dust and rusty equipment lined the walls. Kate peered out to see a dark neighboring home about thirty yards away. "We'll be okay in here," she intoned sternly to the driver. Lightning flashed brightly through the building's thin windows, casting brilliant bursts on the barn's brief inhabitants. The roof rattled from the menacing storm outside.

"What a revolting development." He sighed. "That was quite the action, ma'am." He was impressed with how she'd navigated the door.

"Thank you, it's a—" Kate stopped to avoid any revelations. *No details*, she reminded herself. "It's a gift," she completed her sentence politely. "How are we on time?" she inquired changing the subject effectively.

"It's 12:15 p.m., ma'am. We are about a third of the way back. We should have enough time to wait out the storm and return to the station."

"Well then." Kate sat on a livery trunk and sighed. She did not like to wait. They hadn't passed others on the road to the Mission, and she'd like to keep it that way for the remainder of the trip. The driver cooed to his frightened horse and offered it the better hay. The rain and wind whipped at the barn steadily for an hour. Kate paced uneasily, fanning out her clothes to dry as the driver tended to his horse. It was hard not to speak but even small talk could put them at risk.

When the storm finally passed, the two left the barn in a hurry. They scurried into the wagon like two squirrels preparing for the winter. Overcast skies blanketed them as they drove onto their main route. The carriage abruptly stopped, stuck in a muddy rut. "We have a problem, ma'am," the driver shouted as he jumped down to inspect the carriage.

Oh no, I've got to catch that train. "What's wrong?" Kate hollered back.

"It's mired in muck," he yelled pitifully.

"Do you have any tools?" Kate jumped out to join him, immediately ankle-deep in the thick sludge.

"Yes, I've got a pick and shovel." He grabbed them from a compartment under the carriage seat.

"Alright, let's dig it out then," Kate spoke with pluck. The rear right wheel stuck about a half foot deep into the brown mess. They frantically toiled, pulling the slop away, splattering themselves with the wet mud.

As they had most of the wheel uncovered the driver ranted, "Okay now, let's get her outta here." He jumped atop his perch and slapped the reins. "C'mon boy." The horse started and the ground made a sucking sound, relenting to give up the wheel. The driver cracked his whip and lashed the animal. "Yah, c'mon boy!" The animal snorted and grunted as Kate stood by angrily, gathering up the skirt of her dress with clenched fists.

"Stop!" she shouted. "Give me the reins. Get behind the carriage and with my word, give it a push." The driver grimaced but followed her orders and stood behind the embedded vehicle.

Kate calmly walked to the head of the frustrated horse, reins in hand, and stroked its forehead. "There, there now. You're a strong one. How about motivation?" Kate proffered an apple from her pocket. "Mmm, yummy, eh?" She held the treat up and the horse came in for a bite and she leaned back. "Start pushing!" Kate yelled aside to the driver as the horse trudged forward. Kate led him with the sweet fruit. The encouraged beast pulled the lead tightly. The carriage strained as the driver leaned into it with all his might and broke free. Kate hastily removed his bit. The horse greedily munched into the apple as Kate laughed merrily. "You get more bees with honey than you do with vinegar! Let's go, driver!" Kate readjusted the beast's gear and hopped aboard.

They were off, at last, this time the driver paying close attention to muddier pools in the road. It was past two p.m. and they'd be cutting it close. The horse plodded on through the sticky roads until they approached the town. Kate peered down at her splattered dress and cleaned what she could with her gloves. "Oh bother," she exclaimed aloud.

The sun broke through the clouds just as the coach came to the station with the train pulling up. "Thank you, driver." Kate drew down her veils, popped out of the carriage, and headed for the platform.

Her conductor stepped off just to see his charge approaching. *Oh my*, Porter was amused; she looked as if she'd crashed into a pig sty.

"Good afternoon, ma'am." He took her hand and led her to the first car on the train. "This way, in here." He guided her inside with a firm hand, shut the door, and turned up the gas lamps that illuminated the richly decorated room. Kate was impressed with the ornate car. Rich brown velvet curtains hid the pricey decor from the outside. Several pieces of heavy wood and brass furniture, a private water closet, and a poster bed trimmed with privacy curtains decorated the space. "It appears you encountered a bit of trouble today." Porter twittered at her disheveled dress.

"Yes, the carriage got stuck," Kate murmured, embarrassed by her appearance. But she made it on time, she sighed to herself.

"Obviously," the conductor opined. "Fortunately, we have changes of clothes for you Miss Church." He waved towards a hook on the closet door where two lovely dresses hung. "Accessories and underthings are in the trunk at the foot of the bed. I'll be back for your soiled items later after you've had time to clean up."

"Thank you, and oh…" Kate reached into her bag and handed him the card for Mr. Bartlett. "This is for you."

"Of course, ma'am. I'll be back. Remember our code." He left grinning. She was resourceful and would be well received.

Kate undressed right after Porter left, leaving her filthy clothes in a neat pile. She was itching to be in fresh garments. The clothes stuck to her like glue and made her skin itch uncomfortably. Kate wiped down at the water closet basin and reapplied her powder. The woman in the mirror shocked her. How different she was with dark hair. She ran her fingers through the black locks and admired her reflection. Mission accomplished.

The train rolled off as she chose a dark green high collared piece with forest green ribbons and ruffled trim. There were plenty of underpinnings in the trunk, silken stockings and bloomers, velvet soft gloves, and embroidered corsets.

Kate had just finished dressing, tying on a sturdy, but ladylike set of boots when the familiar knock was heard. The door opened and the conductor entered, bringing a tray with tea and a selection of cheese, fruit, and biscuits. "I thought you might be ready for a snack." He set down the tasty selection of food.

"Yes, thank you, Porter." Her stomach growled in agreement.

"I'll just gather your items then." He reached for the pile of her discarded clothes and then for her parasol.

"Oh. I'll take care of that." Kate pushed away from her seat and picked up her weather-beaten cover. The conductor raised an eyebrow. "It's special," she remarked in a kind but stern tone.

He acknowledged, "As you wish, ma'am, I'll be back later to collect your tray."

"Thank you, sir." She reclined back into the chair with a salacious grin and put down the parasol as the conductor left. *If he only knew how "special" it was*, Kate laughed to herself.

16 THE CIRCUS

Kate was not completely content after eating her snack. Her trip regrettably confirmed her suspicion that Drasco killed Sister Theresa. Now that she had a moment to relax, Kate was haunted by his wicked deeds. Her head ached with a dull pain. Maybe he died in the blast? Could she be so lucky as to be rid of him permanently? But she may never know. She was heading home after a last Engagement. Kate sighed and curiously opened Engagement #2:

"Dear Miss Church:

As you are reading this, I can assume that you have completed your first Engagement. Thank you for your service.

For this Engagement you are simply to observe; you will not participate by any means. The train will arrive in Kansas City at 10:30 a.m. You will wear one of the dresses provided to you, but you must wear a green hat with the pink taffeta roses. As before, a driver will be waiting for you, only this time with a black stagecoach. He will have red roses on his hat.

As before, you are to nod and touch your hat to signal your arrival. Your driver will escort you to your rendezvous, which will be a traveling circus. You are to purchase tickets for the noon trapeze act in the big top tent once you arrive. Be certain to sit on the northern side of the tent where the performers enter the ring.

Strax and the Widow

During the second act of the trapeze performance, the lead and head of the troupe, Mr. Marisi will be announced and approach the bar. Immediately you are to find where the support lines are tethered near the performer's entrance. A young man with a brown newsboy's cap will appear and will cut one of these lines precisely as Mr. Marisi begins his act. He will disappear just as fast. Only observe this act which will result in death or acute injury.

Slowly count to thirty once this event has taken place, then leave the tent and return to your driver who will usher you to the train. Note that panic may ensue. You must remain attentive to your surroundings. Do not pause to aid or become a cause for anyone else's attention. Leave and do not look back. You will not intervene under any circumstances.

You are to confirm that Mr. Marisi has indeed fallen; simply write yes or no on the card to confirm that this action was carried out and give it to your conductor contact as before. Should your driver or conductor not be available for any reason, you are responsible for your safe return to St. Louis. Discretion is of the utmost importance. Be cautious at all times.

Upon your return, your conductor will have further instructions regarding the remainder of your trip.

Thank you sincerely,

W."

Kate had heard of circuses but had never seen one. Interesting, however, she didn't look forward to watching people die. Hadn't she had enough of it? And why only watch? Maybe W. was testing her? He demanded thoroughness and completion. Kate began to question her mercenary missions.

She put the papers away and cracked open her Bible but was distracted by her conscience. There wasn't a place for confession, and she mustn't tell anyone what she was doing now.

How is this of any use? It's a means to an end, she convinced herself, but her mind was rambunctious. The landscape outside faded as the train rolled into darkness. The conductor's precise rap interrupted her musings. "Good evening, dinner will be served shortly." The conductor curiously noted her Bible. "Fresh materials to read until your meal is ready?"

"Yes, that'd be lovely." Kate was grateful for a pleasant distraction and access to news.

Porter left and brought several newspapers, which Kate devoured. It had been weeks since she'd seen any news other than rail papers and W.'s letters. It occurred to her that she'd been living in a shelter for far too long; a violent desert of no comfort, but cover nonetheless. The world seemed to carry on without her. She pined as she read each word before the standard knock announced her meal. "Your dinner ma'am." The conductor set down the tray as Kate tucked the papers away. "I will be back to collect it before nine p.m."

"Thank you," Kate replied and consumed a sumptuous feast of beef with gravy, greens, crisp bread and butter, and hot tea with cream and sugar. It was a fantastic meal; at least her tummy was satisfied. The remainder of the evening was uneventful. Kate just finished reading the various newspapers when the conductor arrived with a lovely gray jacquard hat box.

"This is for tomorrow." He placed a round container by her steamer trunk. "Anything else before you retire?" he inquired kindly.

"No, thank you, sir," a tired Kate replied as the day's earlier events caught up with her.

"Very well then. The train is making a late stop shortly and then will continue through the night to Kansas City. I will return at eight a.m. tomorrow with breakfast. Have a pleasant rest." The conductor waved towards the bed.

"Thank you." Kate felt energized as Porter left. She tidied up, hanging her dresses, and putting her other items out of sight. She undressed but instead of using the nightdress in the steam trunk, she took out the well-worn silken gown given to her by Ming. It smelled of Strax and old linen. Kate fussed, missing her canine friend. She wiped away the warm tears, tucked herself in, and drew the bed curtains shut just as the train made its brief stop. The whistle sounded and the train continued its journey.

She was drifting off to sleep when a singular tap at the door stirred Kate to the core. *Am I dreaming?* Kate sat bolt upright. *Maybe it was an odd noise.*

Then another set of knocks, this time sharper and urgent.

It's the wrong combination, Kate's mind raced. She tugged aside the window curtains next to the bed and as she surmised, a window with moonbeams pouring in.

As a third clunk rattled the door, Kate slid up the sash and climbed out the window of the speeding train. She dare not peer down as the rail ties whipped by in a dizzying fashion. The chilly air slapped her awake and ravaged her hair into a wild frenzy. The thin gown pressed tightly on her skin, providing little protection against the oppressive wind. The cool metal of the outside of the car stunned her hands but Kate managed to keep a sturdy grip. *Hurry, he's coming. And of course, my bag and weaponry are neatly tucked into the steam trunk,* she fretted.

But Kate had been around the rail long enough to know that if she got to the car's ladder, she'd hide up top. As her eyes adjusted, she saw it, an arm's length away. As she strained and caught the sidebar, she heard the interior door to the car open. She swung fully onto the ladder, reached back, shut the window, and scampered to the roof. Her car was next to the engine and coal car. She strained to see the driver attending to his instruments through the smoke and steam. Kate deeply regretted she couldn't ask for his support.

Instead, she balanced, then lay flat on top of the car, her ear pressed heavily along the metal, straining to hear.

Inside, a loathsome man invaded the car. He had been told it was occupied but his knocks went unanswered. He turned up the gas lamps and peered around. There was only a single door to this car, one way in, one way out. Perhaps the woman he was seeking was hiding. He first checked the water closet and found only a couple of clean dresses. The steamer trunk was not large enough to hold a person. He drew aside the bed curtains. "Hmm," he pondered, the covers were askew. She had been in the bed. He felt the linens still warm from her body heat.

And I just missed her, unless, he mused, *she's under the bed.* He knelt and peered under to find nothing.

The intruder paused for a moment. *She couldn't have gone out the window.*

He peered up from the floor to see the bed curtains opened. He leaped onto the bed and threw open the window as the train raced. He searched right and left to no avail. "Drat, surely she hadn't exited this way," he mumbled.

Kate peeked over the edge to view the man's shadow from the window outlined by the gas lamps inside.

Oh no. Where had this bastard come from? She lay completely still, frozen on top of the car in the brisk wind. Chin's voice popped into her head, "You strong now Kate." *I am. I can wait here all night if I have to.*

The man waited. *She couldn't stay out forever if she was indeed outside,* he figured. Ten minutes went by, then twenty. Not a sound, not a sight. He opened the window and leaned towards the ladder, not an easy reach, especially for a woman. But still, he should check.

Kate saw the movement of his shadow. She slid like a snake to the edge of the car and swung over the side just as her pursuer shimmied up the ladder. She perched on the railing on the backside of the car, outside the only door and in between the moving rail cars. Her legs shook with the vibration of the train as she held on with a vise-like grip.

The man shimmed up just enough to the top of the ladder to see that he was correct; nothing was atop the car. He climbed back in. She'd received word that he was coming. She probably took off as he got on. His superiors wouldn't be happy; they had procured intelligence that she was or at least had been on that train since Nacogdoches. He shut the window and exited. He'd have to blend in with the other passengers, at least for overnight. He slipped into the neighboring car. He was so annoyed in not finding the woman that he didn't notice her hiding directly behind the door of the car as he left.

When the interloper shut the door to the passenger car, Kate breathed at last and then crawled in.

What a close call! She bemoaned. She didn't get a good look at her interloper in the dark between the cars but saw just enough to know it wasn't a cowboy, the conductor, or even Mr.

Bartlett. He was of a formidable height and had a bowler, but darkness covered his details.

Although unable to lock the door, Kate deftly braced a chair under the knob. She took out her pistol and whip and brought them to bed with her. She griped that hopefully, this wasn't becoming a habit, as sleep did not come easily that night.

The gentleman of many names arrived in Hermann, Missouri, a lovely German river town, late in the evening. It was a short walk from the train station to a tavern where a saucy barmaid poured him a glass of the local refreshment, a sweet, crisp wine. "Good evening, Mr. King," she greeted him warmly. "I wasn't expecting you'd be back in this direction." Her turquoise eyes twinkled in the low gas lamps. Her golden ringlets danced around her ample cleavage from which she produced an envelope.

"Just passing through." His kind British accent filled her ear as he tucked the note into his coat pocket and took a sip of the beverage before continuing. "Unfortunately, I won't be staying long."

"As you wish." She left and attended to her other guests.

The gentleman tossed back the rest of his drink and walked to a neighboring hotel where he simply nodded to the clerk and headed upstairs to a specific room. He locked the door and sat on the bed, eager to see the envelope's contents. Several tiny photos were just big enough to show the destruction. Several dead from Drasco's gang and three buildings were destroyed. Miss Church took to her flight impulsively. This did not bode well with the other Members.

The gentleman checked his pocket watch, turned out the gaslights, and rested atop the sheets in the dark. "Please do not be too hard, Miss Church," he whispered to himself, hoping that her other Engagements were completed satisfactorily.

Kate awoke with the sunrise and the conductor's knock. She covered herself with a bed sheet and removed the chair as the conductor realized he couldn't open the door. He heard the sliding of furniture as his charge peeped out, then let him in. "Pardon me," she intoned as he twittered at her disheveled appearance. She was lovely, even wrapped in a sheet and dirty old nightdress with her hair undone. "I had a visitor last night."

The conductor froze. "When?" he paled.

"Just after the train stop," Kate sensed his urgency.

"He might be here, on the train. Did he see you? What happened?" The conductor was aghast.

"He didn't know the code. That gave me a few seconds' warning. I climbed out the window and hid alongside the train until he left."

He was impressed at her cleverness but was concerned that this astonishing woman was being pursued by someone that managed to elude the conductor.

"What did he look like? Did you see him?"

"Just a shadow, tall and a bowler hat."

"I'm checking the cars and will bring back breakfast. I see that you're ready." Porter's voice trailed off. Kate gazed down and saw that in her anxiety she was still gripping her pistol and whip over the sheet.

"Um, yes, then. Thank you," she stuttered.

"Take great care while I'm away. We'll have to be vigilant, even after we arrive in Kansas City." She shut the door behind him and then, giggled impetuously.

Oh my, I must be a fright. Kate laughed as she dressed and waited for her morning meal, her weaponry at her side. The conductor returned with the standard tapping and a breakfast of eggs, sliced ham, biscuits, and tea.

"Several men have bowlers on the train. I will come for you after the train stops. Should there be any trouble, we'll react appropriately. Please, stay here until then, ma'am," he directed her. Porter was grateful she was armed and wiser than most other women he'd known.

"Of course, thank you." Kate grimaced as the conductor left. This was unexpected. Agitated, she ran her fingers through her hair, over-styling it for her new hat. They were diligent in tracking her. Kate gazed out the window as the buildings of Kansas City rapidly evolved from the distance. The train stopped and she heard passengers moving throughout the cars.

The conductor departed, scanned the platform, and found Kate's pursuer in short order. He was indeed a tall man wearing a bowler, but the interloper neglected to dust off his crisp white shirt from his brush with the outside of the train. Smudges were apparent to one as observant as Kate's ally. The conductor watched as the mysterious man headed straight for a waiting driver and left immediately.

Porter hurried back to Kate. "Now!" he urged. She was ready, having affixed her designated hat and loaded her bag. He ushered her out and was assured that her driver was across the platform, red roses on his cap.

She passed her signal to him, nodding, and adjusting her head cover.

The driver greeted her warmly, "Good morning, ma'am," and welcomed her into the stagecoach. It was an upgrade from her previous ride. It was fully enclosed with plush brown velvet curtains and tan cowhide seats. This ride was also shorter; within a half-hour, they reached the fairgrounds where the circus was set up. The driver tethered his horse, opened the door, and with a genteel hand, assisted Kate off the coach. She headed immediately into the crowds to purchase her required ticket.

Exotic smells filled the air—plump pigs on spits, grilled corn on the cob, and roasted nuts mixed in with the foul stench of wild animals and their droppings. People bustled happily among red and white striped tents that contained amazing feats by stunning performers. Huge beasts roared and stomped in their immense cages, both terrifying and delighting curious children that dared to peek.

Kate found the ticket booth and stood in line with several other thrill-seekers. She heard a familiar voice; that of a flirty debonair gambler warbling sweet nothings close by. She leaned back to see the familiar profile of Mr. Whitney touching the shoulder of a raven-haired, scantily clad female from behind. The woman turned to face him, her lower visage covered in a full black curly beard, and he gasped in horror. Kate covered her mouth to keep from laughing aloud. As the dejected Mr. Whitney headed in her direction, Kate opened her parasol and turned away as the gambler strode past.

Hmm, he'd moved on obviously, but hasn't changed his wild ways. Kate smirked. She watched him walk to a set of carriages for hire and he departed.

Kate sighed at her close call, bought her ticket, and strolled into the big top as the carny barker urged the guests in. It was a half-hour before show time and the tent was filling rapidly. She surveyed the room and picked a seat with a clear view of the performers' entrance.

The ringmaster arrived with a loud "Ladies and Gentlemen!" as he pounced into the ring announcing, "The Mighty Marisi Family, daredevils of the air!"

The lithe troop of two adults and three adolescents took the center. The younger Marisi's scaled the rope ladders and took to the trapeze bars like virile monkeys. They swung dizzily back and forth for several minutes, somersaulting in the air and catching each other.

As their opening act ended, the eldest Marisi climbed up in a brisk fashion, approaching the trapeze platform. Kate found the performer's entrance and her target. The expected young man in the newsboys' cap was already pulling a knife from his pocket and began slicing into the sturdy support rope.

The Marisi children climbed down, and their mother gazed up anxiously as her husband caught the trapeze bar for his solo act. He pleasantly waved to the crowd, his fitted acrobatic tights showing off his musculature. As he swung out into the open with no net below, the support rope snapped, and the trapeze gave way. An audible gasp rose from the audience. He crashed directly into the big top's thickest wooden support beam and fell limply to the floor below. Kate watched as the perpetrator walked outside, now having completed his job.

A chorus of screams and shouts erupted as the Marisi family gathered around their deceased patriarch. A majority of the crowd ran for the exits as newsmen pressed forward for photos. Genteel ladies fainted and their gentleman counterparts were waving their programs wildly to awake them. Kate sighed, paused for a moment to count to thirty, and let the crowd disperse. The numbers impatiently tumbled through her brain. She stood abruptly, her knees shaking as she headed outside.

The sun was unusually bright; she was queasy and shivered a cold sweat. Kate turned away from the tent exit, hurried behind an empty animal cage, and vomited what food was left from breakfast. She held on tightly to the cage's iron bars as she checked her dress and opened her parasol. Kate gazed around and was pleased that no one witnessed this unfortunate event. She gathered saliva in her mouth, rolled her tongue along her teeth, and spit out the remaining bile that stung the inside of her gums and throat.

Kate had seen men shot, accidentally run over by horses, wagons, even trains, but she'd never seen anyone assassinated so covertly. What purpose did this serve? She was still sick at the sight of the trapeze artist's mangled body, his neck and limbs snapped like brittle twigs. Why did this disturb her? *Act like a lady,* she reminded herself.

Kate hurried to her waiting coach. Her driver jumped down in a flash. "Are you alright, ma'am?" he questioned, noticing her blanched appearance.

"Oh, I'm just dandy, thank you," she feigned pleasantries to the driver. *Really fucking dandy,* Kate pouted angrily and then sat stone still for the return trip to the train. Kate wrote "yes" on the card as instructed, tucked it in her bag, and was grateful that this Engagement had been mercifully short. She had seen enough violence to last a lifetime. And as the stagecoach rolled into the train station, Kate wiped a single tear from her cheek with a delicately gloved hand.

The conductor was waiting for her on the platform. Kate wondered how often he changed trains as she approached yet another magnificent steam engine. "Good day ma'am." Porter ushered her into a lead luxury car. She saw that he transferred her trunk. The car had an identical layout to her previous ride, simply different colors on the upholstery and curtains, this time oranges and reds. She passed the card from her bag to him with shaky hands.

"Can I get you anything?" She appeared unnerved as he took her bag and set it on the steamer trunk.

"Oh yes, a drink. Water if possible." Kate sat and removed her hat.

"And a snack perhaps?" He urged. She was reserved and appeared tired. He was to deliver her in excellent condition. He hadn't seen the stranger from the night before. Kate deserved plenty of undisturbed rest before they arrived in St. Louis.

"Yes, delightful." She grimaced. Her body felt the effects of running away, spying, stress, and being beaten to a pulp.

"I'll be back after the train has started." He exited and upon closing the door, Kate immediately wept. She was homesick for a place she hadn't been in twenty years. The violence of the past several weeks overwhelmed her and rose to the surface of her emotions. She longed for her memories of normality, taking care of her father and Abby with Martha, cooking for the Parkers, and being in the stables with Silas and Michael Parker.

Oh, Michael. Kate closed her eyes and instantly she was on the bank of the pond feeling him on her body. She treasured this memory. It had secretly sustained her through her worst days in Iris.

What if Michael approached me earlier?

She fantasized about their lives together. Marrying, having children. Father getting well. Abby growing up happily.

The steam engine hissed and brought Kate back to reality. She opened her eyes, sighed, and freshened up in the water closet. The conductor's familiar knock came just as she reseated herself. He brought in a tray with water, hot tea, and blueberry scones. The tasty smells made Kate's stomach growl. She was stunned that she was hungry after the day's events. The conductor set the food down. To his relief, she looked better. "Ma'am, I have your final note." He reached inside his waistcoat for a familiar parchment envelope with the red seal. Kate felt uplifted and couldn't wait to read it.

"Thank you." She eagerly took the letter.

"I'll be back at dinner time when we have a stop in Hermann. Then it will be straight through to St. Louis. We'll arrive in the early hours, around seven a.m., I'll have breakfast for you then." The moment he left; Kate opened the last envelope of her trip:

"Dear Miss Church:

Thank you for your exemplary service. A package containing your payment will be delivered to your family home in St. Louis in a few days. As always open it in a private place. Please destroy the information regarding your previous Engagements as soon as possible, preferably by fire. As before, discretion is of the utmost importance. Also enclosed will be a note of where we are to meet within a couple of weeks of your return. I look forward to the discussion of our future endeavors. In the meantime, please rest and enjoy your reunion with your family.

Sincerely,

W."

Kate warmed at the sudden change in fortune.

I'll finally meet the benefactor and have twenty thousand dollars. Is this real?

She buttered a scone and nibbled hungrily as the sun set. Kate ate as she imagined what home was like. She tucked the note in her bag with the others, leaned back in the chair, and unintentionally fell into a nap.

17 HOME

St. Louis, Missouri, October 1895

Abigail Church reread the letter delivered by a kind visitor who now stood in the Church family parlor chatting with Martha. He was dressed in a coal-black vested suit and a crisp bowler, which he held politely at his waist.

"Dear Abby:

The man accompanying this letter, Mr. Ferris Tomley, is preceding my arrival home. I should arrive shortly thereafter. Mr. Tomley has become a well-cherished friend of mine. He is intelligent, kind, and a most perfect gentleman.

My dear sister, I know that you have been unduly burdened in caring for our father since I left, and I pray you can forgive me for my delayed return. I know that you have been lonely and feel that your time as a possible bride is passed. I am writing to tell you that Mr. Tomley desires to be your husband. I have provided him with a sizable dowry, and I am assured that he will be delighted to marry you after asking father's permission, should he be lucid enough to entertain Mr. Tomley upon his arrival.

I hope to come home to find you happily engaged and father in better health!

Your Sister,

Kate"

Abby gazed across the room. The man was a stranger to her. How did Kate just offer her up to this man? But then Ferris grinned at Abby, and she acquiesced.

Kate was right, Ferris mused. She'd told him about Abby, and showed him a picture from months earlier. She had lovely copper ringlets and stunning green eyes like their father. Her porcelain skin had childish freckles that framed her pink lips.

Abby returned his gaze. *My, he is attractive. Why didn't Kate want him? Well, he was too young apparently.*

Her mind was spinning; she took a deep breath, collected herself, and walked as ladylike as possible to her fiancé. "Well, Mr. Tomley, I am encouraged at my sister's insistence, and I know she means well. Perhaps you should meet my father. Let me check upstairs to see if he's awake. Please have a seat. Martha?" She gestured towards her staff and the ladies went upstairs.

Ferris grinned. Abby was feminine and smelled of lavender, like Kate, but she had a genteel sweetness about her. *Thank you, Kate.* He sighed gratefully to himself. The gold ring he'd purchased yesterday was burning a hole in his pocket. He'd barely slept at the hotel before heading out to buy a new suit. Ferris had been waiting for a decent hour to arrive at the Church residence. He didn't want to let Kate down.

Abby and Martha stopped short of Mr. Church's bedroom door and whispered. "Oh Miss Abby, he's a fine young man. Not fantastically tall, but my, did you hear him talk? He's educated and handsome!" Martha gushed.

"Martha, I cannot believe what just happened." Abby felt ready to burst. "He is such a gentleman. He kissed my hand!" She tapped on her father's bedroom door and beamed at Martha. "I can't wait for Kate to get home."

Two days after Ferris had arrived in St. Louis, Kate departed the train and gave a standard nod to her conductor. She was relieved that the rest of the journey home had been completely uneventful. She had slept decently despite her recent crazed travels. She was exhausted, and slumber had come easily.

That morning, Kate peered in the mirror before dressing. The bruises were now an ugly green-yellow, the scrapes a few bare lines, but the whip marks were permanent.

No one will ever see my backside, Kate promised herself.

Kate sighed and dressed in the other gown provided, a simple dark navy dress coat with a suede black collar, cuffs, and buttons. No ostentatious dress. To remain incognito was of the essence until she was contacted by W. An early breakfast had satisfied her as the sun rose over a hilly landscape that rapidly turned from farms to country, to neighborhoods, and finally to a city larger than Kate had remembered. The conductor passed her trunk to a porter. "A driver is prepared to deliver you home. Be safe, ma'am. It was my pleasure."

"Thank you, Porter." She nodded and touched her hat as the new driver saw her.

This escort had signature green feathers tucked into his cap. He was polite and with a quick "Good morning, ma'am," he'd ushered her into the carriage. He tipped the porter and secured her trunk. They started into a beautiful fall day.

How St. Louis had changed in only twenty years. Kate watched in amazement as carriages filled the streets. Ornate buildings seemed to have erupted from the ground in Victorian splendor. Businessmen, dock workers, ladies, and children filled the streets. Soon they'd entered a familiar neighborhood of manor homes.

The carriage turned into a wide cobblestone street lined with grand trees offering their autumn-colored brilliance to the air. It was her street, but the trees were grander, the houses statelier than she'd remembered. After a short ride, they rolled up to No. 3, her childhood home. Kate was awkwardly filled with memories. Field hands were burning leaves and, regretfully, she still felt the flames that had killed Michael Parker and McKendrick. Her back stung in protest and Kate shuddered. Tears came, but she exhaled deeply and pondered the future. "Ma'am, are you ready?" The driver had dismounted, opened the door, and was prepared to support her exit.

"Yes, yes I am." Kate faked pleasantries while emerging into the early morning sun.

Mr. Bartlett departed his carriage onto the Society's immense grounds, the main hall looming in elegant brick and marble. His timepiece pulsed in his pocket reminding him of his appointment. With an intense purpose, he strode straight to the office of Mr. Roth, his footsteps echoing on the fine flooring. An ornate lift took him to the third floor, an area reserved for the most Senior Members of the Society. He made a crisp left down the hall to the wing of the Director, Mr. Roth. He knocked and upon a deep voice urging "Come in" from the other side, Mr. Bartlett opened the exquisitely carved oak double doors to an elaborate office.

Behind a sturdy oak desk, stood an equally solid man, Mr. Alistair Roth. He had neatly trimmed hair with a side part that enhanced his firm jawline. His blue eyes peeked over horn-rimmed spectacles as he perused a file of a female prospect, one familiar to Mr. Bartlett. "Welcome back Christopher. I see you've made it back alive." His voice boomed pleasantly in a slight Irish brogue as Mr. Bartlett closed the doors behind him. They shook hands and sat in the office surrounded by art, books, and files.

"I did indeed, and as of this morning, Miss Church as well." Mr. Bartlett nodded wearily.

"Ah, she is a pistol, isn't she? Clever, smart, but perhaps a touch too strong-willed?" The Director questioned his longtime colleague.

"She can be tamed with training. I have seen her in tender moments. For example, she is extremely kind to children and animals," Mr. Bartlett protested.

"Then again, she blew up a warehouse full of explosives we were ready to procure." Mr. Roth quipped. "She only had to escape. We require an asset, not a destroyer."

"But that demonstrates vision? Proactivity? She didn't know we were procuring the green liquids. Besides, with her investigation, we can now harvest it ourselves. And if we act now, there's only Drasco and a couple of his men left before their reinforcements come in." Bartlett was confident. "We can transfer those cacti here."

"You and your botany." The Director quipped. "That greenhouse of yours welcomes the challenge." He paused to light a pipe. "Alright, we can get a team out to tie up those loose ends. In the meantime, is she prepared? Will she'll accept?"

Mr. Bartlett leaned forward with excitement. "She's perfect. Her father is ill, and she's found a husband for her sister. She has no children, no other attachments. She's fearless; she stood up to a gang of villains several times. She takes direction. She knows horsemanship, and weaponry, and has already proven that she can disguise herself well. She even carries a whip in her bag."

Mr. Roth puffed on his pipe, measuring his friend's enthusiasm, then spoke. "She cleans up well then? Just attractive enough?" He hadn't seen Bartlett this interested in a recruit in a long time. It was hard to find new Members, but did he like her too much?

"Yes, she can act like a lady, and blend into a crowd," Bartlett agreed. "I think that with a generous offer she'd come."

"But for greed?"

"No, for necessity. She's been a provider for a long time. I believe that with a reward, she'd be encouraged. Besides, she has a conscience." Mr. Bartlett remembered his priestly duties and her confessions at the church in Iris.

"Alright then, send her payment and an invitation. When can we expect Miss Church's arrival?" Roth was chomping at the bit to meet this prospect. He was desperately concerned that she could live up to the Society's expectations.

"It should be two weeks at most. This will be enough time for her to settle her family affairs."

"Well then, it's up to you. Please use the appropriate time to recover. You know what they say: 'a weak person cannot complete strong work'." Mr. Roth stood, came round the desk, and slapped Mr. Bartlett's shoulder good-naturedly. His colleague was a gentleman and had been in search of a deserving trainee, a decent partner for a long time. He shouldn't be burned.

Bartlett rose from his chair. "Yes, thank you. I am looking forward to resting at home." Inside he was buoyed with his prospect, yearning to have Miss Church join him.

Kate and Abby wailed like schoolchildren. Ferris stood in amazement at the sisters' reunion. He was just as shocked at Kate's coal-black hair and the dress she wore. She was stunning. The sisters held each other tightly as Martha collapsed into a chair sobbing. They hadn't stopped hugging since Kate had walked in the door. Her driver had dropped off her trunk and left without issue. "Oh, Kate! I can't believe you're here, you're really here!" Abby squealed and kissed her sister's cheek.

"At last, I know," Kate reddened from the excitement. "Oh Abby, you've grown to be pretty." She touched her younger sister's cheek. She was still the cherub she'd left long ago. Kate turned towards Ferris. "I trust you've met my lovely sister?" she joked. Before Ferris spoke, Abby squealed.

"And this!" The younger Miss Church held out her left hand to reveal a shiny gold ring.

"An engagement! How wonderful!" Kate hugged her sister, then crossed the room, and embraced her former manager. She spoke softly in his ear, "Thank you, Ferris, I know you'll be good to her."

"You're a saint, Kate," he whispered back. "I am glad you made it home." Kate turned away and wiped her eyes.

"I'm glad to be back too. Did you..." Kate hesitated; she didn't see her father. "Ask for father's permission?"

"Yes," Ferris replied solemnly.

"Kate, he is severely ill now, in and out of slumber all day. But he was awake, and he approves." Abby was equally somber.

"And today?" Kate inquired.

"The doctor says any day now, he is terribly weak." Abby sniffled. This time sad tears fell.

"Come with me upstairs," Kate ordered as she mentally prepared herself. Ferris remained with Martha in the parlor. She and Abby climbed the stairs, rapped on the bedroom door, tiptoed in, and stood at the bedside in the darkened room.

"Father," Abby whispered, "Kate is home."

Their father was a shell of the man he'd been, painfully thin, and his gray hair had fallen out in patches. He lay on his back covered in fluffy quilts. He moaned in pain, adjusted his eyes, and then smiled at his two girls. "Oh Katie, you have black hair!" He laughed, then coughed.

"Shhh, you don't have to talk." Kate sat on the edge of the bed and stroked his forehead. "I'm sorry I was away for so long." Tears for her father tumbled freely.

"Don't cry, Kate. Abby dear," he choked, "let me talk to your sister in private for a moment."

"Of course." Abby kissed his cheek and left without another word.

Henry Church held his eldest daughter's hand with as tight a grip as he could muster. "Oh, Kate. How you've provided, done the impossible. Please, between us, tell me what happened. Why'd you leave?"

Abby strained to hear outside the bedroom door. Why her sister had kept secrets she'd never known. And when Abby was old enough to suspect a tragedy had happened, she'd asked Martha, but she was stoic with no viable answers. She'd heard whispers about deaths on the Parker's property and that Martha's brother had run off. After a moment of unaccomplished eavesdropping, Abby went back downstairs.

Kate strove to ease the soul of her dying father. *Oh God, forgive me for oversimplifying this,* she intoned. "The day the barn burnt down," she began with a trembling voice, "McKendrick attempted to harm me. Michael Parker stopped him, but not before the barn was set ablaze. Silas was rescued, but McKendrick's brother blamed Silas for the fire, and he ran." Kate sighed.

Her father closed his eyes with satisfaction.

"McKendrick was eyeing you, even before you were becoming a woman," Henry whispered his eyes still shut. "I didn't have the heart to tell Mr. Parker that his most reliable driver didn't have the best of intentions with my daughter. I failed you, Katie. And Silas. That man wouldn't have hurt a flea." Henry coughed and Kate tipped a cup so he could sip water.

"No, father, you couldn't have stopped him. And it's okay, Michael Parker told me he loved me that day and he was asking you for my hand." Kate eased his mind without completely telling the truth. Henry blinked his eyes open.

"Michael was a strapping young soul. That evil bastard McKendrick ruined your life." Henry coughed and Kate patted his chest. "You made hard choices, Kate. I'm sorry I wasn't a better father." Tears came to his tired eyes. Kate clutched him tightly.

"No, papa, you did your best. Don't be sorry, don't be upset. Please rest."

Henry squinted at his eldest daughter. "Promise me you'll see my dear friend, our neighbor Mr. Parker, and offer him closure. He too is ill." His voice faded as he drifted back to sleep. Kate went back to the parlor where Martha was serving tea and biscuits.

"He's resting." Kate sighed.

"Let's have lunch and get you settled in." Abby wondered if she would ever know Kate's secrets as she sat at the table.

After they had eaten, Ferris carried Kate's trunk upstairs, and Martha began to unpack in her childhood bedroom. "Thank you, Ferris." She leaned in for a hug, "I will speak with you later. Please keep my confidence, what happened in Iris, you know."

"Yes, of course," he replied and returned to his fiancée. Kate was grateful to be alone with Martha.

"Miss Kate, you sure travel light." Martha laughed at the small number of items in Kate's trunk.

"Just leave that, I'll do it." Kate took her hand, and they sat on the bed. Kate looked pained with heavy, dark circles under her eyes. "Martha," she gasped.

"Oh, Miss Kate!" she laughed as the women hugged. "We missed you so bad. You'd run off, you were just a girl. And now, you are quite the woman."

"Working for the rail, well, let's just say it was interesting." Kate laughed. "And you, you were just as strong at the worst of times. Have you ever heard from—" Martha stopped Kate with a brief gesture.

"No. Nothing. I ask God daily for his protection." Martha spoke without saying her brother's name.

"Well, after Abby and Ferris are married, you're welcome to go with them. I have enough salary to help you make your own decisions Martha. I owe you that. Silas saved my life that night. You and Silas." Kate grasped her hand tightly. "And you raised Abby, took care of father; I can't repay you enough."

"Miss Kate, you did your share too, and in the middle of nowhere. You're leaving again?" Martha was befuddled upon hearing that Kate hadn't included herself in the Church family plans.

"I have offers to pursue. But for now, I'm visiting Mr. Parker." They hugged and then stood.

"You're a true gentlewoman, Miss Kate. I hope you can stay."

"We'll see." Kate intoned mysteriously. The ladies checked in briefly on Mr. Church who continued to sleep, then returned downstairs. "I'm going out." Kate put on her hat, picked up her parasol, and gazed at her smitten sibling.

"Let's stroll in the park, dear." Ferris swooned over his bride-to-be. Abby giggled in return. Kate was relieved to see that they were already happy. "Care to join us, Kate?"

"No, I think you two wish to be alone." Kate teased. The trio headed outside.

Ferris and Abby left for Lafayette Park, just blocks away. Kate, meanwhile, headed in an opposite direction.

She walked down the street, past the stately mansions and splendid gardens to the Parker grounds. She opened a gate she hadn't passed through in twenty years. Her heart beat faster as she approached the still exquisite mansion and saw Mr. Parker sitting by himself on the expansive porch.

"Hello?" he croaked as he heard the autumn leaves crunching under the feet of an approaching person. His dark spectacled eyes lacked vision, but he smelled a waft of perfume. It was a lady and by the tempo of the steps, a younger one. "Hello?" He leaned forward on his cane and strained to hear.

"Mr. Parker?" Kate inquired as she climbed the steps to the covered porch.

"Kate!" he cried, astonished, recognizing her voice immediately. "Miss Kate Church, is that you?"

"Yes, yes!" She laughed merrily and sat next to him on a fine wicker cushioned sofa. He reached out for her hand, which she offered, and he kissed it.

"Miss Kate, you've come home after such a long time." His voice filled with joy. He was still handsome but frail, just like her father. She wondered if Michael would've aged as well.

"Yes, I'm here. My sister Abby is to be married. And well, father, you know." Her voice saddened.

He tightened his grip.

"I am glad you are home, Kate." He paused. "I know that you have come to tell me something."

Kate exhaled and repeated what she'd told her father, sparing Mr. Parker the gory details of his son's last moments on earth and leaving him with the memory of Michael as a hero. "Oh Kate, you didn't have to run. It was wrong, I just knew it was wrong." He shuddered.

"I had to leave," Kate explained sadly. "I had an opportunity, and I didn't believe I could stay here without Michael." A huge, haunting burden lifted as she revealed the truth.

"Michael loved you." Mr. Parker grimaced. "I'd have been proud to have had you for a daughter-in-law." He began to weep openly. "I am a silly old man." He paused for a moment and inhaled deeply. "Please tell me you are happy now, Kate?"

"Yes, yes. I'm home, no place I'd rather be." Kate agreed and they sat and reminisced until the sun hung low in the sky.

Mr. Parker was at peace, knowing the girl that his son had loved was home safe.

Days after Kate's return, Abby became Mrs. Ferris Tomley, married at the bedside of her father. A week later, Henry Church joined his long-passed spouse in eternal rest. After his daughters had spent hours of each of those remaining days reading him stories, poetry, and Bible passages, he died in his sleep. Mr. Parker deceased a few days later, also satisfied that he'd had closure; that his son had died defending his true love.

The Church household had neighborly visitors with the sudden occurrence of family events, but Kate let her sister shine as the happy new bride. Kate consistently had the reminder "Do not draw attention to oneself" in her head, should she decide to possibly accept an offer from W. It was not time to make new acquaintances. As Kate had planned, Abby was happily distracted by her new husband and didn't question her about Iris. Fortunately, talks of the railroad bored her easily.

Kate and Ferris agreed that no words of the violence of Iris could ever pass between them. The tragedies they'd suffered remained a horrifying secret.

After a week, Kate wasn't sleeping well. Her dreams teased her with memories of her past. She'd awake, her body sweating and hearing laughter, believing it was Drasco. But she'd sit up in bed, only to realize it was Abby and Ferris satisfying their marital desires in the middle of the night. She'd turn over and silently cry herself back to sleep. Early one morning, she came downstairs to see a familiar invitation had been dropped through the post slot in the door. Kate's heart leaped up in her chest with a tingling excitement. It was time to entertain an offer.

Kate sat on an ornate bench on a sunny mid-October morning. Mr. Bartlett had contacted her as promised. The invitation read:

"Dear Miss Church:

Please dress like a lady for a meeting with Mr. Bartlett at Lafayette Park; the third bench north of the Police Station along the eastern path and wall. Tuesday at 10 a.m. He would like to have a Discussion with you about possible opportunities. Your payment for previous services rendered is enclosed. Thank you.

Sincerely,

W."

Kate was thrilled with the pay. But she had a suspicious feeling. Her benefactor seemed to know all about her and as promised, had contacted her upon her return. Her mind was still confounded. She was tired of death and violence. It was wonderful to be home. These conflicts rambled loosely in her brain.

The Tuesday meeting came too soon for Kate. Lafayette Park was filled with residents enjoying the early fall. Children cavorted in the browning grasses as their parents chatted. Leaves turned and dropped their autumnal riches on the earth. It had rained the night before, but the bright blue sky was drying the dewy ground. Kate had indeed dressed like a lady, wearing the navy-blue coatdress, with a matching fascinator and black boots. She'd brought her parasol and a bag that contained her pistol and whip, just in case.

Why had I come? Silly me.

She had completed her tasks and was home; Abby and Ferris were happily married. Father was resting with the angels. A smidgen of the truth had even assisted Mr. Parker in passing on. She relaxed. She was still tired and required rest. Kate had the resources and time to decide what to do. She stared off to the distant trees of the park, enjoying the silence.

As Mr. Bartlett approached, he admired Miss Church's serenity. Perhaps she'd be receptive to what he'd had in mind. "Good day, may I join you?" Mr. Bartlett greeted Kate.

Her eyes widened with surprise as he approached in such a stealthy manner.

"Yes, please do," Kate said simply, ambivalent about what might happen next.

"I trust that you have received payment?" He slid in next to her on the bench. Mr. Bartlett sensed that Kate wasn't quite herself today. He had bet that she'd come round to his offer; her talents were in demand. Her hair was still coal black. It brought out the blue in her eyes and enhanced her pale skin. He was impressed at how well she'd disguised herself.

"Yes, thank you, it was appreciated." Kate turned to him and was taken aback at how attractive he was in the autumn sun. Mr. Bartlett wore a dark vested suit with a fine pocket kerchief tucked nattily in the jacket. The chain of his pocket watch reflected in the sunlight that rippled through the trees. His black bowler shaded his steely eyes.

"Very well then. I first must tell you that I had hoped you'd follow instructions perfectly. Your exit from Iris was brash and drew undue attention, which displeased your benefactor. We can't have these sorts of actions if we are to continue our association."

Kate pursed her lips. He was a perfectionist. Expectations increased over time. Didn't he realize she'd barely escaped?

"Sir, your criticizing is unnerving, and I don't appreciate you admonishing me like a child." Kate snapped. Even in the safety of her childhood home, she'd had night terrors and often cried herself to sleep over her horrible months in Iris. His harsh words felt like a bullet to the head.

"Miss Church, you must know that if we are to proceed, you should realize that all actions cause reactions. Several others may have been hurt by your lack of compliance." His stern tone infuriated Kate and she turned away momentarily.

"People were already harmed. And some I loved are dead." Kate glared back at him. Her hands clutched her bag and parasol in a vise-like grip. *This is bullshit.*

"You agreed to our terms. Going forward, you will have to be circumspect." He was firm but strove to be patient in making her understand the delicacy of each task without explaining everything just yet. She seemed ready to bolt at any moment.

Kate leered at her contact. "I almost died. How dare you make me feel inept?" Her ire welled up, tightening in her chest. *I can't do this,* she fretted, *it hurts too much; I don't even know this man.*

Mr. Bartlett hadn't expected this. Obedient precision was desired. He approached the subject. "I would like—"

Kate stood abruptly, interrupted, and spoke tersely, "I think that I am no longer interested in what you would like. Good day, Mr. Bartlett. It was a pleasure doing business with you." She turned and started down the path. He immediately jumped up in pursuit. He had to avoid drawing outside attention. Mr. Bartlett took her arm from the side and began, "Miss Church—"

"Unhand me!" Kate reacted harshly.

He scanned the crowd to see if anyone was watching. It seemed that the youthful squeals of joy from children playing loudly covered her outburst.

Kate began to walk away, wearing a fierce pout and her arms crossed.

"Miss Church!" he hissed behind her. "Miss Church!"

"Fuck you!" she spat with such fury that she nearly crushed her parasol in her hand. At this moment she did not feel like being a lady.

"Miss Church! Miss Church!" he proceeded through clenched teeth. "Who sent the natives?"

Kate stopped and turned, her mouth open, eyes wide.

"Who sent the Indians?" He spoke forcefully. His eyes held hers in a direct stare.

"No, no, you didn't," Kate stuttered, incredulous. Had he been there when Drasco almost killed her? She was frozen; he had seen it all. But why hadn't he intervened?

"Please, please stop. Listen, just wait a moment." He pulled her aside from the path and whispered, "Please wait and be a lady." Then he grazed his fingers over her cheeks and placed a tender peck on her lips. He held the kiss just long enough for an elderly man to stroll by. He had to tame her for just a moment, to talk sense into her. Mr. Bartlett felt her relax. She had closed her eyes. They opened sleepily when his mouth lifted. The elderly gentleman twittered pleasantly and passed them.

Kate was flummoxed. *Did he just kiss me?* It had been warm and tender. Heat surged through her, and she wondered why men had this strange power.

"Shhh," he whispered pulling her close and gazing over her shoulder at activities in the park. They were still unseen by the crowd. "It's a pity to hear such harsh language from your lovely lips. I did not intend to hurt you, but you must listen, Miss Church. It means your life, do you understand?" he cooed in Kate's ear.

"Yes." She gasped, still in shock from his sudden embrace.

"This is to remain between us." His pleasant British lilt warmed her. "I am sorry that you were in such grave positions. I overheard Drasco's men at the saloon bragging about how they were getting their money back. I couldn't risk it, taking off after you, but I found out where the tribe was located, and I persuaded them to save you." He was still holding her close, his hands on her back, her breasts brushing his chest. "You already rescued one of their own." Mr. Bartlett was intoxicated by the lavender scent on her neck.

"What if they hadn't come? You'd have let me die?" Kate choked, still rattled over the ambush and the violence that had consumed Iris.

"Miss Church, I cannot answer that." His measured words tickled sweetly in her ear. "What matters is that you escaped, and I have another opportunity for you." He released his grip as she had wept silently. "Don't be too soft now, Miss Church, compose yourself." He proffered his handkerchief, and she wiped her tears. "Let us sit down then." He took her hand and led her back to the bench. It was time for a Discussion, and so it began.

"I will apologize that I may have spoken abruptly, Miss Church, but your benefactor is displeased with how you left Iris. However, I know that you have completed the additional tasks he had ordered, and he's offering you a permanent position. Your brashness in using explosives did not bode well with him."

Kate was muddled. *What is this? An inquisition? Or a job offer?*

Mr. Bartlett recognized her confusion. "I assure you, though, he has been notified of your capabilities and believes you're right for the job."

His gaze eased and Kate allowed him to continue. "I must be firm. There will be moments of extremely demanding work, like the ones you've already performed, but you will be rewarded handsomely. You will see things unimaginable, places you've dreamed of. Everything will be provided by your benefactor: your room, food, clothing, all fine, luxurious things. You will want for nothing. However, once you agree to terms, you cannot go back to how you once lived. You will have to leave your family and friends behind."

Kate was aghast. She'd just arrived back home and finally felt a sense of normality.

Mr. Bartlett saw hesitation. "We must have a sincere commitment, Miss Church. As long as men like Drasco are in the world, we must act for the greater good. If you were to return, you'd put yourself in harm's way."

Kate was stunned. That bastard was still alive, and hadn't she already been in peril? She inhaled deeply and sighed. "I presumed I was meeting Mr. W today."

Mr. Bartlett heard the dejection in her voice. "I understand your disappointment, but he has been called away on an urgent matter. Your benefactor has been impressed with your performance and he will be available once you've made a decision." If she only knew how much W needed her; the gentlemen thought. "Of course, an opportunity of this importance should be taken with the utmost caution. You have two weeks from today to decide. I will contact you for us to discuss your answer."

Kate's heart thumped so loudly that she surely thought he heard it through her chest.

"I, I don't know what to say," she stuttered. This was completely unexpected. She had the impression that they were hiring a secretary or clerk.

Kate stared into the distance while Mr. Bartlett fretted about her fussing too much over his offer.

"Miss Church." He reached for her hand and stroked it. "Please, a moment." Her eyes moistened with tears. "Now, now don't be too soft." His voice was clear but kind. "I know that you are stronger than that."

Kate's mind was cleared as if she had heard Chin say it to her before.

He gazed into Kate's eyes.

Kate felt as if he read her mind and steadied herself, daring to glare back at him.

"The decision is yours, but I promise you, it will be the adventure of a lifetime." He was hypnotizing, sincere as the night they first met.

"Alright then, I will be ready with my answer in the time allotted," Kate responded firmly.

There was personal business to handle first, she mused with clarity for the first time since they had met that morning. "What about my family? Mr. Tomley, my brother-in-law will require employment. And their servant, Martha, has a lost brother. She is without kin and is growing old."

"Her brother's name?" the gentleman inquired, ready to negotiate.

"Silas. He escaped with the Underground Railroad in Alton about twenty years ago. I can give the address from where he was emancipated," Kate offered.

"That could be arranged." Mr. Bartlett was measuring the request carefully. This was unexpected bartering, but he had to have her, no matter what it took. "Write down the address on this card after you return home." He proffered W's reply cards from a waistcoat pocket. "I'll have a courier pick it up tomorrow."

"Thank you. I appreciate it." Kate felt a growing comfort as they sat together.

"Very well then, I will send a calling card for our next meeting in two weeks." He stood, kissed her hand, and assisted her from the bench. "Thank you, Miss Church, good day." His eyes hadn't left her face. From the looks of it, he believed that the future was in his favor.

"Thank you, Mr. Bartlett. I will see you then. Good day." Kate opened her parasol and left. Kate was peculiarly elated. She already had her answer, or did she? Kate did indeed have tasks to handle before deciding.

The gentleman watched until she had passed out of his sight. He hoped the next weeks passed without incident. He was certain that the lady had arrived at her destination. He sat back on the bench, took out his timepiece which had pulsed, and checked the time.

The pocket watch was engraved with "For the greater good. L.C.W." He closed the cover and was ready to return home to a stunning manor. It was on the grounds of a greater compound, the Society, where he was known by his true name, Lord Christopher Wilson. Kate had unknowingly already met her benefactor. Lord Wilson counted on her return so that his identity could be revealed. He stood, returned to his waiting carriage, and mused that he'd like to share more than just future Engagements with Kate Church. Perhaps even his darkest secrets, all in due time.

The End

Book One of The Society Trilogy

Strax and the Widow

BOOKS FROM VICTORIA L. SZULC

More works (and future releases) by Victoria L. Szulc:

The Society Trilogy (a steampunk series, revised):
Book 1-Strax and the Widow
Book 2-Revenge and Machinery
Book 3-From Lafayette to London

More Society Steampunk Stories (revised):
A Long Reign, The Society Travelers Series, v.1
The Kicho, The Dolls of Society, v.1
A Dream of Emerald Skies, A Young Society Series, v.1

The Brown Lady, Short Story Edition

The Vampire's Little Black Book Series (revised): v. 1-15

The Vermilion Countess Series

A Book of Sleepy Dogs

ABOUT THE AUTHOR

Victoria L. Szulc is a multi-media artist and author. Victoria's work has been recognized in St. Louis Magazine (2019 A-List Reader's Choice Author 2nd Place winner), Amazon UK Storytellers 2017 semi-finalist, the Museum of the Dog, and her illustrations of Cecilia for "Cecilia's Tale" won a runners up award for The Distinctive Cat Stephen Memorial Award 2019.

Inspired by the works of Beatrix Potter, the Bronte sisters, Jane Austen, C.S. Lewis, and Ian Fleming, she "lives" her art through various hobbies including: drawing, writing, volunteering for animal charities, yoga, voice over work, and weather spotting. She specializes in pet portraiture through her company The Haute Hen.

For character development she's currently learning/researching chess, fencing and whip cracking. Victoria blogs about these adventures at: mysteampunkproject.wordpress.com

and

https://haute-hen-countess.square.site/

"Adventures abound and romance is to be had."

-Victoria

Made in the USA
Monee, IL
27 August 2022